THE FEARLESS GROOM

TEXAS TITAN ROMANCES

CAMI CHECKETTS

BIRCH RIVER PUBLISHING

COPYRIGHT

The Fearless Groom: Texas Titans Romance

Copyright © 2017 by Cami Checketts

All rights reserved.

DEDICATION

To my amazing group of writing friends: Taylor Hart, Jennifer Youngblood, Lucy McConnell, Cindy Roland Anderson, Jeanette Lewis, Christine Kersey, Rachelle J. Christensen, Kimberly Krey, Daniel Coleman, Kimberley Mont-petit, and Sarah Gay.
I love that you understand that my characters are real people and don't tease me for living in my head with Peter Pan and the Tooth Fairy. Thank you for the support, the wisdom, and the laughter.

FOREWORD

Dear Reader,

"Work isn't WORK unless you would rather be DOING something else."

~Don Shula, Miami Dolphins

When I saw this quote, I instantly thought of the three authors of the Texas Titan Romance series, Cami Checketts, Taylor Hart, and Jennifer Youngblood. They work, day after day, to create swoon-worthy romances, characters to fall in love with, and a world where pure love can bloom. It ain't easy folks! Yet, I know they get up in the morning with the thought, "I *get* to be a writer today."

So much of football, or any sport, is a mental game. If you're head's not on right, then you're not going to be there for your teammates when they need you. These ladies are the ones I want on my team. They are fun and creative and they are serious business women with goals and deadlines. They come through. Every. Time.

That's why, when they told me about their new football romances, I could see them scoring a touchdown by writing books that would inspire readers to sigh, laugh, and fall in love with the game all over again. That's just what they've done. I'm thrilled to introduce the

Texas Titan Romance series—I know you're going to get lost in the pages and have a great time.

I hope you enjoy The Fearless Groom by Cami Checketts, The Persistent Groom by Jennifer Youngblood, and The Tough Love Groom by Taylor Hart.

Happy reading,

Lucy McConnell, author of the <u>Lime Peak Ranch Series</u>

INTRODUCTION

Like the mythical Greek God's who played on Mount Olympus, the men on the **Texas Titan Football** team are larger than life. More heroic, tender, and gorgeous then should be allowed!

But the reason I love these men has nothing to do with their looks or how they throw a ball or catch a pass. It has everything to do with their passion—on and off the field.

The stories about these men are like unwrapping your favorite candy and letting it unfold slowly in your mouth, filling your taste buds with joy and wonder...until it's gone...and you have to reach for another. They're addicting!

Xavier Newton is the kind of man who knows what he wants and goes after it. Of course his best quality is also his most infuriating! I loved reading this story and watching how he and Izzy fall in love!

Get ready for sizzling romance and an emotional journey that will have you turning page after page late into the night!

Taylor Hart

Author of *The Tough Love Groom: Texas Titan Romances*

Hello Fabulous Reader,

Let me begin by saying that if this is your first time reading one of Cami's books, you're in for a treat! If you've read her work before, then you already know how wonderful her stories are. Cami has a way of drawing the reader in from the first page. And boy, oh, boy, does she know how to create chemistry between the characters! When *I read The Fearless Groom,* I found myself smiling thinking, *Dang, I wish I'd written that!*

Cami is not only a wonderful writer, but also a great person. She's always the first to offer a kind word or to cheer someone else on. We need more Cami Checketts in this world, and I feel very blessed to call her friend.

Pull up a comfy chair ... and enjoy this delightful, fast-paced, spunky story that kept me flipping pages to find out how it would end.

Cheers,

Jennifer Youngblood

Author of *The Persistent Groom: Texas Titan Romances*

FREE BOOK

Sign up for Cami's newsletter and receive a free ebook copy of *The Feisty One: A Billionaire Bride Pact Romance* at www.camicheketts.com.

1

Isabella Knight pasted on her smile and waved to the cluster of photographers as she walked up the sidewalk and through the arched doorway into the Rosecrest Mansion. Unfortunately, the beautiful Spanish architecture with the warm yellow stucco exterior, clay roof tiles, and arched windows and doors was lost on her. She was too busy checking the location of her security detail for the night. Two nondescript men in tuxes followed her at a discreet distance. She scowled then immediately smoothed her face out when another camera flashed. This was exactly why she tried to avoid social media. Somebody at the hospital would usually show her when a particularly unflattering photo hit the Internet.

Thankfully, her regular life as a nurse practitioner didn't include over-muscled goons following her around, but they were forced on her at any large social gatherings she attended. She often told her half-sister they weren't the ones in danger. It was their father who was the money-grubbing tycoon. The threat was all on him. Still, she was smart enough to realize that kidnapping her or Hailey would be profitable for someone. Her father had enough parental inclinations to pay a ransom for Hailey, though she wasn't a hundred percent certain about herself.

Clearing the doorway, she glanced back one more time to see if her security guys were following and waved to the swarm of photographers again. She looked the part of the daughter of a wealthy oil tycoon and the owner of the Texas Titans. She wore a form-fitting teal blue knee-length dress and gorgeous Manolo Blahnik silver heels. Her father's clothing designer had not been happy when she insisted on capped sleeves and no exposed chest, but the dress was tight enough that every bump and curve was on display for the world to ogle and dissect.

Turning forward, her eyes widened as she realized a broad back encased in a navy-blue suit was right in her path. She lifted her hands to keep from planting her face in between his shoulder blades and grabbed onto two very defined arms. Whoa. Whoever this guy was, he was more built than her bodyguards.

"Excuse me," she said, letting go and stepping back, but the point of her two-inch heel caught between one of the tiles of the floor, and she was going down. Arms flailing, she prayed with everything in her she was far enough inside the mansion that the paparazzi, who had been banned to the outside, were not capturing what was sure to be the worst moment she'd had in a decade.

The man pivoted, saw her wind-milling limbs, and caught her in one fluid motion. Izzy was suspended in mid-air, a foot away from the floor, staring up into deep brown eyes. They seemed to look straight into her, pulling away all the crap the world had tried to pump in there and seeing the real her—her heartache for the pain she saw children going through, her hopes of being enough to help them, and her hidden desire to not do it alone.

She pushed out a long breath. The man smiled, and she could see his five-o'clock shadow wasn't grown out enough to hide a perfect set of dimples. Her heart slammed against her chest. Xavier Newton. Oh, crap, this was *not* the first impression she wanted to make.

"You all right, ma'am?" he asked, gently lifting her onto her feet, but keeping one hand on the small of her lower back. His palm was nice and big, perfect for snatching footballs out of the air and making her go hot and cold all over.

"Thanks to you." She found herself returning the smile with a genuine one of her own, nothing close to the plastic version she'd been giving the photographers and reporters out front.

"Glad to be of service."

"With muscles that big, you probably catch a lot of things. You're just a big old hero, aren't you?" Izzy was horrified those words had just come out of her mouth. She may have been a natural smart aleck, but she tried to not flirt with good-looking men unless she knew them well enough to be assured they weren't philanderers like her father. Xavier Newton sadly only fit in the good-looking category.

His smile deepened, and then he chuckled. "I try, ma'am. I surely do." He turned her down the hallway and toward the main area where the gala and auction were being held. "Can I escort you in?"

Izzy bit at her lip. Her father would be thrilled at this turn of events as this was the man he had specifically instructed her to buy like Xavier Newton was some kind of horse or long-horned steer. It made her sick the way her father had said it, but he'd also given her unlimited access to his charity fund if she promised to win the bid on Xavier. All that money was going to her beloved children's hospital, so it was one of the few times he knew he had her over a barrel.

Xavier was a member of the Triple Threat, the three top football players in the nation and the heroes of their Texas Titans football team. Tonight, he was up on the auction block as one of the eligible bachelors. The prize was a date with the man himself. Izzy sucked in a breath as she looked at him—six foot four and full of muscle with smooth, brown skin and sculpted facial features. He'd made *The Rising Star's* "Most Handsome Men" list five years running. It wasn't just that he was easy on the eyes. It was also those irresistible dimples and the story of him rising from poverty. Not to mention, he treated his mama like gold. What woman didn't love that? He flew her to every home game, remodeled her home because she refused to move from her downtown Denver neighborhood, and bragged about her anytime anyone asked. He seemed perfect. Well, except for the fact that he dated and dumped women faster than Izzy could complete a shift at work.

Izzy realized he was staring at her with an arched eyebrow, and she still hadn't answered his question about escorting her in. "Um, sure, that would be ... delectable."

"Delectable?" They walked slowly down the hall, and Izzy knew people were staring at the two of them together. Did Xavier know she was the owner's daughter?

"I mean, nice." Had she truly just said delectable to Xavier Newton? She shouldn't be flirting with this man, but couldn't seem to help herself. There was something different about Xavier ... something she wouldn't mind exploring.

He grinned again. "Sitting with you at dinner would be delectable."

Izzy blushed, grateful her skin was dark enough he probably wouldn't notice. "I don't think we get that choice." They entered the room, and she pointed at the setup. The head table had only three seats. Kade Kincaid, Ace Sanchez, and Xavier Newton were the guests of honor and were expected to be on display for all the hungry women waiting to bid on them and claim their right to a date with one of the superheroes. Izzy wondered how out of control the bidding was going to get.

"No, really?" He shook his head. "I hate these things."

She looked him over. His tailored navy-blue suit perfectly encased his lithe frame, and his face was exquisite, with manly lines, deep brown eyes, and dimples everyone died over. She knew the women would be lining up to bid on him. She couldn't help but smile. She would win that bid because her father had instructed her to, and the money would all go to her beloved hospital. Her smile fell as she wondered for the hundredth time why her father had been so insistent she bid on Xavier. This whole thing was going to go viral. Maybe her father just wanted more exposure for his precious football team. He thrived on exposure. *Please, please don't let the press have seen my near fall and Xavier's catch.* She laughed. He really was good at catching things. Then she realized Xavier was studying her with a quizzical expression. Oh my. He was going to think she was a nut job and beg someone else to bid on him.

"Your face is very expressive," Xavier said. "But I'm not sure if you agree with me about the absurdity of these sort of events or if you're laughing at me."

"I'm sorry. I was just thinking I hope the photographers out front didn't get pictures of my near-fall and your catch." She clasped her hands together and admitted, "And then I was thinking about how good you are at catching things." A mental image of his glorious biceps as he stretched out to catch a ball had her biting at her lip again.

Xavier smiled. "Catching you was more fun than any football I've snagged."

"Oh, really?" She put a hand on her hip and tossed her long, dark curls. "More fun than catching the winning touchdown pass from Kade Kincaid at the Championship Game?"

He chuckled, and those dimples were so irresistible she wanted to touch them. She refrained, barely. "Okay, you got me there. A different kind of fun." He leaned closer, and she was blessed with a whiff of his cologne—some kind of delectable mix of lime, musk, and salt. There she went, again, thinking how *delectable* he was. It was a word one of her young patients had used recently. It had cracked her up, and now, she couldn't get it out of her head, especially in relation to Xavier.

"But I'd catch you any day of the week," he said in a low tone reserved just for her.

Izzy almost fell so he could catch her in those nicely-built arms again. She settled for fluttering her eyelashes. "Maybe you'll get a chance later."

He chuckled again, removed his hand from her lower back, and stuck it out for a handshake, all formal-like. "I'm Xavier Newton. It's a pleasure to meet you, ma'am."

Izzy was the one laughing now. "The pleasure is mine, Mr. Newton." She put her hand in his. Instead of shaking it, he simply held onto it.

"And you are?"

"Izzy."

"Just Izzy?"

She couldn't give him her last name. She wasn't ready for that. Sure, Knight was a common enough name, but he had to know the owner of his team's name, and he could easily put the connection together if he hadn't already recognized her. The local media liked to broadcast pictures of her occasionally. She wasn't nationally acclaimed for being the daughter who'd dumped her billionaire father, but in Texas, she was a household face and name.

"You have to earn a last name, football star." She gave a saucy little shake, shocking herself again. Was she losing all her inhibitions? Her mother had been a fabulous salsa dancer, and Izzy had dreamed of following in her footsteps, but her father had only ever agreed to ballet, getting a sad look in his eyes every time she begged to dance salsa or mamba as a little girl. Izzy hadn't truly danced in years.

Xavier's eyes widened, but he grinned more broadly. "I hope I get a chance to earn it. Who are you here with, Izzy?"

She recognized exactly what he was saying. How did she afford to pay five thousand dollars for this dinner, and who had invited her, or was she here on her own merits? Oh my, she'd completely forgotten about her security. She glanced around, but they were blending in with other security personnel surrounding the walls. They must've realized Xavier Newton wasn't a threat, not physically at least. He was about to make her have an emotional seizure, holding her hand and flirting with her.

"I'm a nurse for the Dallas Children's Hospital. I understand you hate these events, but we're very grateful you are willing to donate your body, I mean, a date for the children."

Xavier laughed, but sadly released her hand. Her fingers felt instant remorse. "I'd do anything for the children, but I hope it's just a date. Not ready to donate my body yet."

"X!" Kade Kincaid yelled across the room. "Get over here."

Xavier glanced over his shoulder at his buddy and lifted his index finger, signaling for one more minute.

"You're being summoned," she said.

"Sorry," he said to her. "When Kade Kincaid wants something, he usually gets it."

"I've seen that."

"Do you watch our games?" He suddenly looked like an adorable boy asking if his favorite friend was going to support him at little league.

"Every single one." She assured him. "Who could miss the Triple Threat?"

"Thanks. That means a lot." He cleared his throat and shifted closer. "Could I offer you a ride home after the event?"

Izzy's heart slammed into her chest. It was just a ride, but it felt like much more. Would he still want to take her home after she'd bought him like cattle on the auction block? Something was really bugging her about her father being so gracious with his money for the hospital on the condition that she buy Xavier.

"I don't take rides from someone I've just met." She folded her arms under her chest and lifted an eyebrow.

Xavier's eyes dipped for just a second, but they quickly came back up to focus on hers. "That's a shame. Here I am selling my body, I mean, a date for your hospital, but you can't make the sacrifice of a simple ride?"

He had her. Oh, man, did he have her. The thought of him selling that body brought heat to her neck. "So riding home with you would be a sacrifice?"

"Depends on where we go on the ride." He smirked and gave her a suggestive look that had her panting for air.

Izzy put a hand on his chest and tried to push at him. Unfortunately, he didn't budge, but the sculpted muscles of his chest felt sumptuous under her fingertips. "I'll have you know that I'm a good Christian girl, and we won't be going *anywhere* for a ride." She pinned him with a look.

A laugh bubbled out of his chest. She could feel it and hear it. He wrapped his large palm around hers. "I like you, Izzy with no last name. At least wait for me after. We can ... talk."

Izzy pulled her hand free, not ready to make any promises. He'd quickly reminded her that he was a player in every sense of the word, and that was not the type of man she was looking for, ever. She'd buy him at the auction because it would help her hospital, but if he thought he was getting action on that date, he had another thing coming.

"I don't ... talk." She flipped her hair. "Goodbye, Mr. Newton." She strode away angrily, not an easy feat in these stupid heels.

"X!" She heard Kade call again. She made the mistake of glancing back at him when she reached her assigned table. He was watching her with a bemused expression like she was a toy he would like to have fun with. Well, she was nobody's toy, no matter how successful, famous, and handsome they were. Especially when they were all of those things. Her father could be described as two of those three things, and he'd only brought misery to her and her mother, heaven rest her soul. Izzy would stay safe and far away from men like Xavier Newton. At least, she would after she got through tonight and the date she would be purchasing. Hopefully, Xavier would only want to go to dinner in a very public place, and she could just put on a fake smile and soldier through. Too much time spent alone with that man would spell a lot of trouble for her, and trouble wasn't something she had time or energy for.

2

—————

Xavier joked with Ace, but his palms were sweating so much he couldn't have caught a ball if the Championship Game depended on it. He was struggling to cut the perfectly cooked meat in front of him. It was medium rare and probably fifty dollars a steak, and he couldn't even enjoy it. Kade had disappeared, chasing after the pretty redhead he'd had his eye on and Xavier really wished both of his friends were here.

He glanced around the room, searching for Kade. Several women winked at him. A few others licked their lips, and most of them were staring at him or one of his buddies. Most of these same women all had men at their side. He hated these events because he hated people who promenaded their wealth. Silly to say, now that he was insanely wealthy, but he still felt like that kid growing up in Colfax, the west side of downtown Denver, just wishing he could find somebody to toss a football with him and hoping to avoid drugs and gangs and to keep his mama safe.

Finally, Kade walked back in, waving to the crowd and poised as ever. He settled down next to Xavier, cut a bite of meat and asked, "You picked out a little hottie you're hoping will bid on you?"

"Not yet." Xavier leaned back in his chair and grinned, looking like the overconfident player his agent had worked hard to build up in the world's eyes. Even though Xavier hated all the fake dates and publicity, he supposed his agent's plan had worked. His contract was up this year, and he was a free agent. The Titans and Denver Storm were fighting over him, both throwing out increasingly ridiculous numbers. His agent was eating it up and claiming it was all because of the image he'd created for Xavier.

Xavier would love to go home to Denver. He felt compelled to be there for his mama and his little buddy, Marcos. Marcos was an eight-year-old Mama watched out for when Marcos' mom worked late. The kid was already being targeted by gangs and drug runners. Yet Xavier was torn, not wanting to leave Texas and break up the Triple Threat. He loved these guys like brothers.

His eyes perused the room again and landed on the beauty in the teal blue dress who had fallen into his arms on the way in. "Okay, maybe one," he said to Kade.

She looked up, and their eyes met. Something deep and true passed between them, and not for the first time, Xavier cursed his agent for making him look like a womanizer. Izzy had definitely cooled off when he flirted with her, and it was probably because she thought he was a huge player. Little did anyone know his agent set up most of his dates, and they never lasted past coffee and dessert.

"Point her out." Kade urged him.

Xavier lowered his voice. "Spanish beauty, teal blue dress, about your two o'clock."

To his surprise, instead of giving his approval or razzing him that Xavier could never get a date with someone that exquisitely beautiful, Kade burst out a short laugh. "Dude! Do you know who she is?"

Xavier straightened, blinked a couple of times. "Izzy. A nurse at the children's hospital."

"Oh, man." Kade was laughing too hard to explain.

While Xavier waited very impatiently for an explanation, the singer America Starr and the comedian Malcolm took the stage. America started praising everyone for being there and then spent a full minute reminding them their generous donations went to help all the "darling children." She was a child herself, so Xavier thought that line fell a little flat and seemed funny. When she started gushing about the hot bachelors, he didn't find it funny at all. Xavier, Ace, and Kade had all eyes on them. Kade stopped laughing and smiled cockily at the crowd.

Xavier needed to know who Izzy really was. What had he missed?

Ace was on the chopping block first, and Xavier could only hope he didn't appear as cagey and uncomfortable as Ace. Then again, who was he to judge? His palms were already producing their own sweat bank, and he kept wiping them on the cloth napkin on his lap. He didn't hold out much hope of someone delectable, like the beautiful Izzy, being able to bid on him. It would have to be some ridiculously wealthy chick. Then he'd spend the night of the date with her talking about Prada, Gucci, Hermes, or maybe Manolo Blahnik's latest shoes and which parts of Europe or Asia were his favorite to visit. His brow creased just thinking about it, but he'd been on hundreds of said dates. What was one more if it helped children?

"Dude, smile." Kade admonished him.

Xavier forced a grin and noticed a few women titter at him. Honestly, curse the dimples. "Tell me about Izzy," he said in a harsh undertone. He was going to thump Kade after this was over for laughing instead of giving him the details he needed.

"Later, you're up." He nudged him.

A beautiful brunette in a skimpy red dress had purchased Ace for three hundred and twenty thousand dollars. Sheesh. Ace flashed a perfunctory smile, looking pleased about it on the outside, but Xavier didn't think that was really the case. Ace had almost as big of a chip on his shoulder regarding wealthy people as Xavier did.

Malcolm told a few jokes and got the crowd roaring. Then America turned Xavier's way with a predatory grin on her face. Xavier wanted to recoil but kept his smile in place. What was she, all of seventeen years old and made up like a streetwalker? He prayed he had only sons.

"Get your handsome self on up here." America cooed at him. Xavier's thigh muscles flexed as he stood, and he heard a sigh from some nearby women. He'd been idolized for his receiving yards, he knew women loved the stupid dimples, and most of his dates were a sham, but he'd never felt quite so demeaned as he did right now. Suddenly, he was a piece of property to be ogled over and bid on, not a man who had feelings. Okay, he wasn't some touchy-feely guy, but he was a human being with a mind. All for the sake of football. Curse his agent and curse the owner, James Knight, for making them do this.

Xavier strode to the platform, towering over America even in her ridiculous shoes. Izzy's shoes had a decent heel on them, but they simply flattered her. She was a nice height, probably five six or seven, without the heels. America looked like a little girl playing dress up compared to the mature, classy Izzy.

He grinned at the crowd, raising a hand. Quite a few people waved back at him.

"Yes, show off those dimples for us." America clapped her hands around the mic. "Ladies, how could you possibly resist this glorious man?" She licked her lips, and he wondered how that thick red goop stayed on. "Yummy!"

The crowd tittered, and half of the women looked like they wanted to sink their teeth into him. He glanced over to Izzy's table. Her face looked as disgusted with America's diatribe as he felt. Their eyes caught, and all the other nonsense fell away. Izzy gave him an innocent smile, and he realized what he hadn't been able to put his finger on. She was different than all the women his agent lined him up with because she hadn't pushed to initiate something when he'd offered to take her on a drive. She was beautiful and innocent. But Kade had said there was something about her. Something that had his friend cackling at him. What was it?

The bidding started, and Xavier forced himself to break eye contact with Izzy and smile at the women who were bidding on him. They started the bidding at fifty grand. For one stinking date! At least, it was going to help Izzy's hospital. That thought made posturing up here and the dread he felt about going on one more date that meant nothing to him more endurable. His eyes bobbed from woman to woman as they threw their little auction fans up to bid on him. There were quite a few battling it out at first. Some were quite beautiful and some obviously past their prime and kind of terrifying to him. The way their eyes perused his body repulsed him.

When the bidding approached two hundred grand, he felt sick to his stomach. He shouldn't have attempted to eat that steak. How could they just throw around money like this? He could've rebuilt his entire neighborhood for two hundred thousand dollars growing up. *It's for a good cause. It's for a good cause.*

The bidding was down to two women now—a twenty-something platinum blonde with a voluptuous figure that you couldn't miss in her miniscule black dress and a seventy-year-old grandma. The older lady looked classy in a peach business suit and smiled kindly at him, like she might actually be here to donate this money to charity. Maybe she wanted to give the time spent with Xavier to her ten-year-old grandson who loved football. A guy could hope, right?

"Five hundred thousand dollars." The voice rang out clear and beautiful and from the corner where Izzy had been sitting simply watching him be bid on moments earlier.

The entire room seemed to cease all movement and sound. Xavier looked over, and to his amazement and happiness, Izzy sat with her shapely legs crossed and her bidding fan up in the air. She met his gaze and gave him a brief smile before glancing back to America.

The singer's mouth gaped open. She finally snapped her jaw back into place and said, "Well, we've got a new bidder on the floor, my friends, and a very generous one to boot." She glanced at the other two women. "Do I hear five-twenty-five?" Her voice squeaked as if even she realized the absurdity of the number.

Everyone else in the room was still staring in shock, including Xavier. That was more than the price of a home, and for a date with him? And Izzy? A nurse? What on earth was going on? He wanted to go pin Kade down and rap on his chest until he told Xavier what he knew about this woman that had him laughing so hard a few minutes ago.

Xavier stared at Izzy with a questioning look. She arched an eyebrow and simply lowered her hand, setting the fan on the white tablecloth and placing her fingers in her lap. Her face wasn't flirtatious or warm now. It was oddly businesslike. He felt like he'd been tackled by Brady Giles, the two hundred and fifty pound defensive end from New England.

"Ladies?" America tried again, probably thinking she might as well go for more money if they were willing. The pause was long and awkward. Xavier hated James Knight, the team owner, for requiring him to be here, and he hated everyone in this room, except Ace and Kade, for thinking he was their entertainment. Might as well put on a gladiator costume and go chop off some heads. No, these people would probably prefer he dressed like Magic Mike and strip. It was disgusting, and he was fed up. Then he realized he was going to get to go on a date with Izzy. He'd definitely felt something when they were talking earlier, and she was exquisitely beautiful and seemed to have a head on her shoulders, but something was off about her, and until he got Kade alone, he wouldn't know what it was.

"And this handsome bachelor, Xavier Newton, goes to the lovely Isabella Knight."

Knight? Knight? It couldn't be. His jaw tightened. That would explain where she got five hundred grand to throw around. He stared at her, but Izzy wasn't looking at him now, focused on America like she was ready for more entertainment.

A young man in a tux approached the stage and handed Malcolm a piece of paper. He flipped it open and read quickly. His eyes widened. "Oh, Izzy, you are going to love this, girlfriend. Ladies and gentlemen, in case you didn't know James Knight is Izzy's illustrious father. You might have heard of him—owner of the Texas Titans and Knight Oil and Enterprise." He paused, and everyone chuckled. "Mr. Knight wanted to surprise his beloved daughter. You see, Izzy is a nurse practitioner for Dallas Children's Hospital." He waited again, and the room oohed appropriately. "Mr. Knight, knowing how much his daughter loves her hospital, has just offered to donate double whatever Izzy bid tonight. A million dollars! How about that?"

The cheering was loud and unanimous. Xavier had no clue what his face was doing, but if it was as upset as the rest of him, he sure hoped the paparazzi hadn't snuck in here. Isabella Knight. The owner's daughter. The same owner who had picked Xavier up for way below what his agent thought he was worth, but now was willing to pay whatever it took to keep him in Dallas and keep the Triple Threat together. He'd really thought Izzy was different from the usual pampered girls. Obviously not.

The cheering finally died down, and Xavier started to walk away. At least, his time in the limelight was over, but now, he had to plan a date for him and Izzy. The thought would've thrilled him an hour ago.

"Whoa, whoa, stud. Slow down there." America had a hold of the back of his suit coat, and the crowd was laughing now. "We need to hear what you think about all of this." He turned to her, and she jammed the microphone into his mouth.

Xavier forced a smile. "I think it's great. Such a worthy cause, and I'm glad to hear that I play for an owner who cares about children as much as I do."

Everyone smiled and many clapped their approval. It was well known that his mama had started charities for children at home and abroad and he funded them all.

He tried to walk away again.

"One more question." America had a hold of his arm now. "What are you going to plan for the lovely Miss Knight?" America winked at him as if he was going to take Izzy off to some skanky hotel.

Xavier found his gaze drawn to Izzy again. Her smile was tentative and almost as beautiful as the rest of her. Unfortunately, beauty didn't matter a whole lot when you were a snake in the grass. He'd been lured into a lot of uncomfortable and dangerous situations, from preschool on up, but he had the feeling this one was going to be one of the worst. A brilliant thought struck him. He'd teach the rich girl a lesson and enjoy every second of it. Take her to a scummy restaurant and maybe a tractor pull or the paintball experience he, Ace, and Kade had rented out for the team a few weeks ago. That would be fabulous. Shoot her right between those beautiful brown eyes. Eyes that were staring expectantly at him.

"Oh, don't worry. It'll be a date our beautiful princess will never forget." He gave her a snarky smile and stormed off the stage. Let her interpret that any way she wanted to. Ace held out his fist as he reached the safety of their table, and Xavier gave it a bump. Kade stood and waved as the crowd exploded with expectant joy for their beloved quarterback, giving Xavier a manly backslap hug on his way past. "Sorry, man. I should've told you," he muttered.

"It's good." He let Kade go and relaxed into his seat. When he looked up, Izzy was staring at him.

"Sorry." She mouthed.

Xavier leaned back in his chair and zeroed in on her. She thought she'd get off the hook with a lame sorry? This was only the beginning. He arched both eyebrows at her and gave her what he hoped was a smoldering look. If she was one-tenth as innocent as he'd originally thought, she should be crawling in her skin right now. He was going to make her think he was the wolf about to devour the delicious chicken. The joke would be on her when he took her on the craziest redneck date of her life. He was going to be extra careful not to touch her though. All the heat he had felt earlier tonight could not happen with a princess like Isabella Knight.

She returned his look with a smirk of her own. Xavier hated to admit it, but he kind of liked the challenge in her eyes. Let the games begin.

3

Izzy couldn't draw her eyes away from Xavier as he reclined casually in his chair and dared her with a searing look to become one of his floozies. There'd been a moment there where she'd glimpsed an uncertainty and purity that had drawn her in much more than his good looks, talent, or fame would ever do. But it had disappeared, and now, he was the hot ladies' man who planned on treating her like every other plaything he dated.

Her eyes narrowed, and she looked down at the exquisite raspberry cheesecake in front of her. She'd only taken a couple of bites before the bidding on Xavier had started. There was little hope of finishing it now. Her father had matched the five hundred grand. That innocent little girl part of her that used to idolize her daddy, before he'd grown cold and awkward with her and then she found out what a cheating louse he was, wondered if he was trying to show that he cared about her, about the children she'd dedicated her life to.

The grown-up woman knew better. There was an angle here. It might even just be a publicity stunt. She could see it now, "Owner donates exorbitant amount to Dallas Children's Hospital because he adores his daughter."

She didn't think that was it. The Triple Threat gave her father plenty of publicity. What was his angle? She didn't want it to come out. It would just be another reason to hate him.

Loud cheering broke out, and she snapped out of her reverie. The bidding on Kade Kincaid must've just ended. He was teasing with America and beaming for the crowd. Malcolm made a few jokes and some kind of thank you speech that America echoed. Then, thankfully, the event was over.

Izzy started to stand. The young man on her right, who had been trying to keep her attention all evening, pulled out her chair. She thanked him. Robert, that was it. He was a medical student at TCU and the grandson of some U.S. senator she couldn't name right now.

"I thoroughly enjoyed our conversation tonight," Robert said. "Could I bother you for your number and take you to dinner sometime?"

"Oh, I ..." He seemed like a decent young man and it'd been fun to reminisce about medical school, but she wasn't really interested.

"The lady is only going to dinner with one man." The deep voice came from right behind her.

She whirled and found herself face to neck with Xavier. "Now, you hold on a minute," she protested, leaning back to glare at him.

"You bought me sweetheart. Don't go trying to backpedal now." He nodded to Robert, who suddenly looked like a little kid. "If you'll excuse us." Xavier placed his large hand on the small of her back and directed her away from the table, leaving all the people staring at them.

"Goodnight," Izzy murmured, trying to maintain some decorum. She allowed Xavier to escort her out of the ballroom and down the hall, but when he tried to steer her into a small corridor with the obvious intention of finding some privacy, she halted. "Now you see here. I am not one of your little hotties." Where were her stinking bodyguards when she needed them? Probably under instruction from her father to let Xavier Newton have any time alone with her he wanted.

"I think you're plenty hot." His eyes roved over her before he smirked and arched an eyebrow. "You're the one who bought me lock, stock, and barrel." He took a step closer, and she backed into the wall. Resting his arm next to her head, he leaned close. Dang if he didn't smell divine. "What are you going to do with me now?"

She pushed at his chest, but he wasn't going anywhere unless he wanted to. "I only bought you for the hospital."

"Yeah, I figured that, with Daddy's money." He lifted his free hand and trailed it down her cheek.

Izzy lost all rational thought. Her blood felt like it was boiling, and she couldn't concentrate on anything but his closeness and the feel of his fingers on the sensitive skin of her face.

"Now, what I'm trying to figure out"—his voice went low and gravelly, and he leaned dangerously close—"is if you bought me because of Daddy, or if you've got some secret desires of your own."

That snapped her back to reality. He didn't know how close to the truth he was on both points. Izzy ducked under his arm and stepped a respectable distance away. "Everything I did was for the children, but I can't say the same for you." She gave her hair a saucy flip. "You can just forget about the date mister because I have no desire to be alone with the likes of you."

Xavier straightened away from the wall and took a step closer again. Izzy held her ground, refusing to back away and show him she couldn't handle his closeness, his smell, or the predatory gleam in his eyes. She could see why he was labeled a playboy, and she had no desire to give into him, but my, oh my, it was tempting. She had a lot of sympathy for every woman who fell under his power.

"You owe me a date, Miss Knight. I'll pick you up Saturday morning at nine. Wear something you can get dirty in." His dimples deepened.

"I ... owe *you*?" She pointed at herself then at him. "I'm the one that paid for the date, and I get to decide what we do, and if we even go at all."

"I don't think so." He took another blasted step, and his body was overshadowing and overpowering her. She glared at him and refused to back up one inch. "We both know your daddy paid for this date, and I'm not letting you weasel out of it now. I could've had a perfectly nice date with Grandma in there or the plastic blonde."

Izzy had to smile at that.

"You owe me, and I'll see you Saturday." He gave her a smug look and then brushed by her, the quick touch of his body sending shock waves through hers.

Izzy hurried out into the main hall and watched him go. He stormed to the front door, bumping into Ace Sanchez on his way. They spoke quickly. Ace looked back in her direction before walking with Xavier out the tall double doors. Izzy imagined they'd make quite the sensation, two of the three most eligible and good-looking bachelors in the city.

She sagged against the wall, placing a hand to her heart. Had that really just happened? With Xavier Newton? She didn't know if she liked him or not. Her body certainly reacted to him, but that didn't mean anything. He had been cute with her before the bidding, but after, it was obvious he was trying to intimidate and upset her. He must've been mad when he found out who she was. There was nothing for it but to get through Saturday. She didn't want her dad to rescind the funds he'd offered to her hospital—a million dollars. She did a little dance just thinking about that. No matter what Saturday brought, tonight had been more than worth it. Now, if only she could get the smell of Xavier's cologne out of her head.

She was safely back in the car her father had sent for the night when her phone rang. She pushed out a frustrated breath. Think of the devil, and he shall call.

"Hello?" she said tartly.

"Hi, sweetheart. How did the dinner and auction go?"

He'd always called her sweetheart. Even in those years after her mother died when he'd shrunk away from her like she caused him physical pain, whenever he addressed her it was sweetheart. As a teenager she'd fire back that she'd never be his sweetheart. As she'd grown into adulthood, she let it slide. If he wanted to pretend they had a relationship for publicity's sake, she really didn't care.

"Fine. Thank you for your generous contributions." It was stiff, but at least she'd said it.

"Of course. I'm right proud of you, sweetheart, and all you do for the children."

"Thank you," she muttered again.

"Everything went well with Xavier?"

Xavier. Her heart thumped against her chest. She couldn't tell if things had gone well or to pot. It didn't matter. She'd done her part, and her father had been more than generous with funds for her hospital. Again, all she had to do was get through Saturday. "Fine. We're going out Saturday."

"Oh, good. Have a great time, sweetheart."

What did he care if she spent time with Xavier or enjoyed it? She heard a scuffle. Then her stepmom's voice came on the line. "Oh, my love, isn't Xavier Newton the cutest thing you've ever seen?" Dolly squealed. "Mercy me, those dimples!"

Izzy couldn't help but smile, imagining Dolly's hand going over her generous bosom. Izzy had tried through the years to hate her stepmom and half-sister for all that they represented of her father cheating, but it wasn't possible. Dolly and Hailey were the most genuine and loving blonde bombshells she'd ever met in her life. Her stepmom truly looked like Dolly Parton and took great pride in it and she loved Izzy, her dad, and Hailey so much it sparkled out of her. How did someone resist pure love?

"I don't know if I'd say cute," Izzy said, "but he's definitely easy on the eyes."

"He's a stu-ud. Oh, you're going to have so much fun on this date. I told your daddy—"

There was another scuffle for the phone. It happened any time these two called, and it was kind of endearing. Well, on Dolly's part, it was.

"Dolly was just telling me how she hopes you'll enjoy yourself because you work too hard."

Izzy couldn't help but bristle. She worked hard because she loved the children and because she'd cut herself off from him. She took a calming breath. The choice to cut herself off had been hers. There had been many anonymous donations to her checking and savings accounts throughout her college years. She always donated them to charity. At least he did try, in his own twisted way.

The car pulled up to her condo gate. "I've got to go. Give Dolly my love."

"I will. Love you, sweetheart."

Izzy hung up. Yes, she had to give him credit for trying, but mistakes like his weren't easily forgiven.

4

Izzy finished her rounds Friday evening after nine, but she wanted to say goodnight to her little buddy, Jake, before leaving. He had cardiomyopathy, a progressive weakening of the heart muscle, that had grown worse until the point where he needed a donor. She prayed with him every night for a donor to be found. His parents were great but had three older children, and it made it hard for them to be there as much as they liked.

She reached for the door, but a hand on her arm stopped her. She glanced up at one of the oncologists, Dr. Murphy. She'd worked rotations with him a few times, but he made her a little uncomfortable. Most of the other single nurses thought he looked like a model with his bright blue eyes, tan skin, and blond hair, but she wasn't drawn to him. For some reason, she thought about her date with Xavier tomorrow, and her insides pitched with excitement.

"I noticed you just finished your rounds," Dr. Murphy said.

Her skin crawled. Why would he be tracking her like that?

"I'd love to take you out." He licked his lips. "Do you like steak?"

"I'm sorry. It's not going to work for me."

His eyes narrowed. The sparkly blue the women raved about seemed pretty dull to her. "I didn't mention a day yet."

"None of them work for me." She reached for the door handle again. "If you'll excuse me."

"It's all over the internet that you bought a date with Xavier Newton for a million dollars. Pretty high price for a male escort."

Izzy jerked farther away from him. "My father donated a million dollars to help the children in this hospital and to help their parents pay for over-priced slimeball doctors like you."

"Xavier Newton doesn't want an ice queen who thinks she's better than any man. He'll spit you back out so quick your head will spin."

"Xavier Newton doesn't stand a chance with me. Maybe the two of you should get together. You have something in common."

With that, she flung the door open and hurried in. She took a quick breath to calm herself, inhaling antiseptic and stale air.

Jake had a wide smile for her like always. Izzy walked to his bed and gave him a hug, avoiding his oxygen and IV tubes. "How was your day?"

"Boring. The homework specialist came." He wrinkled his nose. At seven, he wasn't picking up on reading yet, and it was torturous for him. At least he liked math. "Can we play a game of Ripple after you pray for me?"

"Sure." Her heart felt heavy though. She didn't feel worthy of prayer with how mean she'd just been to Dr. Murphy. Surely, he had a heart. It just hurt to hear that the doctors and male nurses were still calling her an ice queen or saying she had ice in her veins behind her back. She much preferred Xavier calling her princess. "Would you mind offering the prayer tonight?"

"If you'll play until one of us scores a hundred."

"Deal."

They clasped hands, and he started praying. This was why she had chosen her profession. Jerks like Dr. Murphy and flirts like Xavier Newton couldn't touch her when she was with the children.

5

Xavier had spent the past day and a half trying not to think about Izzy, but unfortunately, his brain was consumed with the memory of the spicy way she'd responded to him, the fluid way she moved on those heels, and the way it had felt when he touched her and got close enough to pick up her sweet gardenia scent. It didn't help that he was in his off-season and wasn't as busy as usual. He was spending his time running, biking, swimming, lifting weights, and dealing with all the paperwork from sponsors, his agent, and the charities his mama had spearheaded. He and Mama were leaving tomorrow for Monterrey, Mexico to spend time in one of the orphanages they funded. It would be good to get away and not think about Izzy or contract negotiations.

Though thinking about Izzy did give him a break from worrying about whether he should accept the offer from the Denver Storm or not. He'd love to play with Cameron Cruz and Hyde Metcalf and live close to his mama and watch out for Marcos, but he, Ace, and Kade had become as close as brothers. How could he bail out on them like that?

This morning, he'd woken up early and run ten miles to ease the jitters. He shouldn't be nervous about this date. He'd dated models, actresses, and wealthy socialites. Isabella Knight was no different. Yet as he showered then threw on a blue Henley and gray golf-type shorts, he knew that Izzy was definitely different. He carefully gelled his hair and trimmed his perfect five-o'clock shadow. It was silly, but when you heard thousands of times how your perfect facial hair and dimples made women insane, you made sure they looked good when you were going on a date with your dream woman. He scoffed. Definitely not his dream woman. The owner's daughter. A liar who'd pretended she was just a nurse. Was she even a nurse? Who knew? He ripped his phone out of his pocket and googled Isabella Knight, staring far too long at her beautiful face. Her mother must've been one of the most beautiful women in the world because her father definitely wasn't very attractive. He looked like he'd gone through so much stress in his life that the worry lines were permanently carved into his skin. There was a commanding presence about the man, and most people seemed to love him, but Xavier wondered what he'd been through to have his face look that haggard.

Xavier blew out a breath. It wasn't like him to be judgmental, coming from nothing and being raised by a mama who was as generous as she was strict. For some reason, Mr. Knight rubbed him the wrong way, especially when they met last. He had insisted that Xavier wouldn't consider leaving Dallas for Denver, as if Xavier had no brain in his head to make a decision and Denver was a slum or something. Okay, downtown Denver where Xavier had been raised was pretty sketchy but so was downtown Dallas.

He glanced around his five thousand-square-foot home in the uppity area The Reserve. It was a sprawling open floor plan with two stories and massive windows and skylights bringing in all the Texas sun he could handle. He'd actually bought it because Kade insisted they all be neighbors and had gotten them in when the neighborhood was being developed. Xavier loved it here. His one-acre, wooded lot gave him shade from the heat and the ability to keep his blinds open and enjoy the outside. The decorator had done a good job making the home similar to a beach house with seafoam walls that contrasted well with the deep distressed cherry wood cabinets and trim. It was manly, yet beautiful. If only he could get his mama to move here, and in an ideal world bring Marcos and his mother with her, life would be just about perfect. Yet his mama felt her place was helping out in the old neighborhood. At least, he'd been able to fix up and build onto her home, expand her yard, and stock her bank account with plenty of money so she could spend it doing good.

Heading for the garage, he debated only a few seconds before jumping in the black Land Rover instead of the silver Bugatti Veyron. He doubted Princess Izzy, as he'd taken to calling her in his head, would much enjoy the day he had planned, but he was going to have a lot of fun with it.

The P.R. department from the team had been great to give him Izzy's address. He wondered if she'd stand him up. She probably didn't even know he had her address and phone number. He should text her, but it was going to be perfect showing up at her condo unexpectedly. He could hardly wait to see her beautiful face, no, he meant the surprise on her face.

———

Izzy paced around the small living area of her condo. It was five minutes to nine, and she debated between barricading herself in her bedroom and running outside to see if Xavier was coming. He hadn't asked for her address or phone number so maybe he had just thought it was funny to claim he was coming and then stand her up. She wouldn't put much past him the way he had teased her. Her cheeks burned remembering how attracted she'd been to him when he leaned in close. Everything he'd said and done showed he was the outrageous flirt the media made him out to be, but Izzy had been pulled in by his spell like any other woman would be. Those eyes and dimples. Lord have mercy.

A loud rap assaulted the front door. Izzy jumped, placing a hand to her heart. She glanced down at her tank top and cargo shorts. He'd said something she could get dirty in. Swallowing hard, she crossed to the door and swung it wide. Xavier filled up the doorframe with all of his deliciousness. Dressed in a blue Henley shirt and gray shorts, he looked as good as he had in his suit. His eyes perused her, and when he smiled, she had to hold her heart again. Darn those dimples.

"You look like you're ready to get dirty," he said instead of hello.

"Such a compliment."

"It is." He placed a hand on the doorframe and leaned closer. He'd perfected that move for sure. "I didn't know if Princess Izzy had ever had dirt under her nails."

Izzy had never been so tempted to hit somebody. "I'll have you know I worked as an LPN at an assisted living center to get through my schooling. You ever cleaned up an eighty-year-old man who defecated all over himself?" She flushed as she finished her retort. It hadn't been the elderly people's fault, and they had been so sweet she'd never begrudged helping them maintain their dignity.

Xavier leaned back. "So you truly are a nurse? That wasn't just a lie to make me fall under your spell."

"I never lie ..." She blinked up at him. His deep brown eyes were soft right now, not as guarded as they'd first been. "You fell under my spell?" Oh my. Was he being truthful? She wasn't a flirt or someone who tried to pull men in, but having Xavier feel that way about her wasn't something she was going to complain about.

He cleared his throat and stepped back. "You ready to go? Lots of fun activities to fit in today. Do you have a change of clothes?"

Izzy hid a smile. Maybe the famous Xavier Newton wasn't as impervious as he acted. She liked the thought of him being under her spell. She grabbed a small bag next to the entry table with a change of clothes, lotion, lip gloss, mascara, her phone, and a credit card. Not that she thought Xavier would strand her without money, but she wanted to be prepared.

They walked along the outside balcony and down the one flight of stairs. Her condo wasn't super fancy, but there was a gate and security. "How did you get in without calling me?" she asked.

"I'm Xavier Newton." He winked cockily.

"Yes, you are." She shook her head. He'd called her princess, but he was the one with the silver platter in front of him now. Interesting, how their roles in life had apparently flipped. She'd been born to privilege and given it up. He'd been born with very little and had made himself a huge success.

He hurried around to the passenger side of a black Land Rover and swung open the door. "Princess," he murmured.

"You need to stop calling me that."

"But it fits so well."

"You don't know me. I can get as dirty as you want me to get."

His eyes widened. A sudden, alluring smile made his face all the more handsome. "I'm glad to hear that."

"I didn't mean it like ... Whatever." She hopped into the vehicle and slapped her seat belt into place. Her face burned. She was no princess or easy woman. By the end of the date, he'd figure it out.

6

Xavier had the XM radio tuned to classic rock. He hummed along with *Sweet Home Alabama* as he drove to the paintball arena. Izzy was definitely fun and unpredictable. He'd give her that. In some ways, he wondered if he should be nicer to her, but she was the one who'd lied to him and bought him with her daddy's money, so the guilt went away pretty quickly. Yet, his mama expected him to treat every woman with respect, and he always did. His dating streaks never went as long as the women wanted them to, but he was kind to them before and after he told them goodbye.

"I didn't figure you for a Lynyrd Skynyrd fan," Izzy said, sitting primly next to him.

He grinned over at her, impressed she knew who Lynyrd Skynyrd was. She definitely had latched onto all those etiquette lessons and looked every bit a princess, even in her casual clothes that she claimed she could get dirty in. His grin deepened. He liked teasing her.

"Guess they didn't have classic rock at your high-dollar private schools," he said.

"No, but we all jammed out in our dorms at night." She practically flung the words at him.

"I would've liked to see that." Then he was imagining her in a nightgown dancing around the dorm, and he had to force that thought away. "You move like a dancer—very fluid and beautiful."

"Oh, thank you." Her voice was full of surprise at the compliment. "I took ballet for fifteen years."

"Fifteen years?" He whistled. "That takes a lot of discipline. So no desire to dance the mamba or salsa or whatever dance they do in, what's that show all the girls love?"

"*Dirty Dancing*?"

He snapped his fingers. "Yeah, that's it. I need to see that sometime." He winked at her.

She stiffened. Her mother had been one of the best salsa dancers ever, and *Dirty Dancing* had been their movie. Of course, her father had knocked all the happiness and dancing out of her mother with his cheating. "Why do you ask? You know how to dance?" She gave him a sidelong glance.

He chuckled. "Malia tried to teach me. She said I was pretty good."

Of course. He'd dated the woman who'd won *Dancing with the Icons* a few years ago and was now a co-host of the show. Izzy should thank him for reminding her that he was just another cocky player. With her dad owning the Titans since she was a teenager, she'd come across her fair share of muscle heads.

"What? No spicy response?"

"I don't think you want to hear what's going on in my head."

"I do. Truly." His eyes left the road for a second and zeroed in on her. She got the sense he actually did want to know, but if the celebrity gossip was even one percent correct, he was too much of a flirt for her to be interested in him. If she ever settled down, it would be with a nice, solid man who didn't even know how to tease or look at another woman. Boring, safe, and if possible, zero chance of infidelity. She'd repeat that a hundred times and hopefully she could stop flirting with Xavier or dreaming of something she'd never have.

"No, you don't," she said. "You wouldn't be half so cocky if you knew what I really thought."

They pulled into the parking lot of Fun N Run Paintball Park. Xavier put his sport utility in park and stared at her. Izzy ignored him and looked around. There was a collection of rusty train shipping containers stacked in her view. The containers were covered with graffiti and formed haphazard two to three story buildings circling the edge of the dirt parking lot. Hopefully they were for hiding behind not climbing into.

"So this is how you're going to get me dirty?" she asked.

"We'll see which one of us isn't half so cocky after today."

She couldn't help but laugh at him throwing that back in her face. She flung open her door and jumped down, not waiting for him to get it.

"Hey." He protested, exiting the vehicle quickly and coming around to her side. "I do have standards for my dates."

She glanced up into his dark brown eyes. "Such as?"

"I get the door, I pay, and I always get a kiss on the first date." His dimples deepened, and she knew temptation had never been so blatantly enticing.

"I guess I can live with the first two, but don't plan on the third."

He moistened his lips and moved a little closer. His musky cologne wrapped around her, and she couldn't quite think straight.

"You sure?" he asked. "I've heard I'm a pretty good kisser."

"You should be! You have enough experience to make that kind of claim." Her face flushed with anger thinking about all the women he'd probably kissed and most likely hadn't stopped at kissing. She suddenly wanted more than anything to get through this date and be done with it. She moved to walk around him, but he wrapped his large palm around her upper arm. Her arm heated up from the simple touch, and she found her gaze drawn to his again.

"You shouldn't believe every rumor you hear, Princess." His voice was dangerously low, and Izzy got a little pleasure out of knowing she affected him too.

"What else am I supposed to believe?" She challenged him with an imperious glare. If he wanted a princess, she could easily give him one.

"Maybe believe that I'm a good guy who just wants to play football, and if I'm really lucky ..." His dimples deepened even without his signature grin. "Maybe I'll find a beautiful princess to kiss."

The look in his eyes had her spellbound. She couldn't move and didn't want to. He leaned down, and before she could escape or protest, he wrapped a hand around her lower back, drew her roughly to him, and kissed her more intensely than she'd ever been kissed. His lips were warm, demanding, and absolutely wonderful. His body, pressed against hers, had her humming with desire. Those large palms seemed to have a mind of their own, as one gently caressed her lower back and the other traced along her neck then tangled itself in her hair. She never wanted his touch or his kiss to end.

Regrettably, he pulled back and stared down at her. She felt she could see into his soul at the moment. That he wasn't the ladies' man the media had made him out to be. That he was innocent and good and ... kissing her when he hardly knew her! He was every bit as promiscuous as she'd feared and no gentleman.

Her hand darted up, and she slapped him across the cheek. He didn't move, and she was pretty sure it had hurt her hand worse than it'd hurt him. Finally, he pursed his lips, nodded, and took a step back, his hands dropping away from her.

"Guess I deserved that."

"You'd better bet your philandering hands you did. Don't ever kiss me again. I'm not one of your little ... followers who want everything you've got to give."

Xavier's eyes shuttered. "Excuse me while I go buy the tickets." He pivoted and left her standing there, walking to a booth with a teenage kid manning it. The young man's mouth was gaping open when he saw who was coming, or possibly he had witnessed the kiss, the slap, and her outburst.

Izzy wrapped her arms around herself and took long, slow breaths. Xavier Newton had just kissed her. Really, truly kissed her. She didn't know if her heart would ever recover.

———

XAVIER'S HEART THUMPED LOUDLY, AS IF HE'D JUST SNAGGED A HAIL Mary over a defender's head and sprinted in for a touchdown. Izzy, Izzy, Izzy. How could one woman be so beautiful, intriguing, and infuriating? Maybe it was true that she'd bought him at the auction for her hospital, not for some ulterior motive that her father probably had, but how could he know? Contrary to what the public believed, he wasn't a playboy, and that kiss had rocked him to the core.

He'd planned this date to try to ruffle her feathers, and he'd sworn to himself he wouldn't touch her. *Way to blow that one out of the water, X.* The need to get to know her better was stronger than the urge to work out every day so he could be on top of his game. He still didn't like who her father was, but was that really her fault? His own father had overdosed when Xavier was three, so he had no memories of him. It was one of the few subjects his mama didn't like to talk about, but he knew better than anyone that you weren't necessarily like your parents.

His thoughts quickly swung back to that kiss. Kissing her had been powerful and overwhelming. She fit perfectly in his arms, and he loved that she smelled like a sweet flower. Then she'd slapped him. He should be ticked, but it actually made him smile. He liked her spice. Yes, the objective of this date definitely needed to change. The focus now was on charming Princess Izzy and seeing exactly what made her tick. It wasn't going to be possible to keep his hands to himself, and he didn't even want to try.

"Hello, Mr. Newton," the kid at the ticket booth said, his fingers tapping quickly on the wooden counter. "We've got everything set up for you, sir, just like you asked."

"Thanks." Xavier smiled to try to calm the teenager down and handed over his credit card. "Are you going to be part of the paintball game?"

"Y-yes, sir." The young man took the credit card, ran it quickly, and placed a receipt in front of him to sign.

Xavier scribbled his signature quick. "Great. It's going to be fun."

The kid nodded vigorously. Xavier wanted to get back to Izzy, but he liked how this teenager seemed nervous and not cocky or begging him for a signature. "Do you want me to sign something for you?" Xavier asked.

"Would you?" The kid's jaw dropped. "Oh, thank you, sir. My boss made me promise not to bug you or stare at you creepy or anything, but you're my favorite player. Honestly."

Xavier grinned and took the football and permanent marker the young man produced. This kid was prepared. "What's your name?"

"Tyson."

Xavier wrote a lot more carefully than when he'd signed the receipt. *To Tyson. Play hard. Pray hard. Xavier Newton.*

Tyson took the ball reverently. "Thank you again, sir."

"Sure thing. Thanks for keeping my coming here quiet." As a NFL star, his every footstep wasn't dogged by paparazzi like a Hollywood star would have to deal with, but there were still plenty of photographs out there circulating about him. He wanted to keep this date just between him and Izzy.

"Oh, of course, sir. We're honored to have you."

Xavier couldn't help but chuckle. He loved fans. He hadn't even looked at the receipt, but he knew he was paying a pretty penny to rent out the whole facility and rent ten of the staff members to play a couple games of paintball with him and Izzy. He didn't want to deal with people off the street who might make a fuss about him. The staff had been instructed to play and have fun with the game and to treat Xavier and Izzy like any other customer.

He jogged back to Izzy. She was pacing next to the Land Rover.

"Okay, they're all ready for us," he said.

Izzy rounded on him and wagged a finger in his face. "And I'll have you know that I *never* kiss on the first date."

She looked so cute, and sadly upset, that he didn't know what the appropriate response was.

"Furthermore, I'll thank you to keep your hands and lips to yourself." She continued, getting up in his face. "I have standards, unlike the women you usually date. You will treat me with respect, or I'll call an Uber."

"Oh, really?" Now she was ticking him off. She didn't know

anything about the women he dated. Sure some of them were ready to undress him before the opening scene of a movie, but he'd dated some really nice ladies too. Plus, Izzy had wanted that kiss as much as he had. "So none of this?" He grasped her hips between his hands and yanked her against his chest. He'd meant to startle her out of her self-righteous diatribe, but the effect on him was strong, his body heating up with desire.

She planted her hands on his chest, and his breath shortened.

"I'm, uh ..." She drew in a shaky breath. "What was I saying?"

"You're calling an Uber." He reminded her, tilting up his chin defiantly.

"That's right," she said all prim and grumpy. But her hands not only stayed on his chest, they stinking squeezed his pec muscles.

"Well, if you're going to ditch me, I might as well give you a reason to." He bent his head and claimed those full lips with his own again.

She let out a sweet little moan then ran her hands up his chest and to his cheeks, cupping his face between her delicate hands. She pulled back and whispered, "I love your dimples." Then she was kissing him again, her arms flung around his neck, pressing up into him as he held her tight.

He finally decided he'd better stop pushing his luck and released her. They were both breathing heavily. "Are you going to slap me again?" he asked, knowing this time he might deserve it. He didn't know her very well, and their relationship so far had been fire and ice, yet he couldn't seem to stop kissing her. He liked to think he had better self-control than he was showing today.

"I should." She shook her head and stepped back. Xavier's hands dropped to his sides, and it felt worse than fumbling the football. "I can't be kissing someone like you."

"Like me?" Well, that was hurtful. She obviously had a different ethnic background like him, and he hadn't figured her for a bigot. "African-American?" he asked tightly.

"No." She pushed at his shoulder. "You're such a dork. No, not that. Because you're a pimp daddy player who goes through women like they're chewing gum."

Xavier took a calming breath. Blast his agent and his stupid career plans—look like you're a big star, and you'll be a big star. Blah, blah, blah. It was all for the image and more money. Now his top two teams were fighting over him, so it had worked, but when he finally met someone he wanted to kiss and get to know better, it made life a sticky mess.

He glanced away from her beautiful face, trying to think how to explain. What would she believe? The entire staff waited at the entry, all geared up and watching them. Izzy's gaze followed his. "We'd better go. You've set up this fun date and all." But she sounded so sad. She'd wanted him to refute her comment. He could feel it.

She turned toward the entrance. Xavier caught her hand and stopped her. She glanced up, and those soulful brown eyes reeled him right in.

"Izzy, please don't believe everything the media shows."

"If I believed even one-hundredth of it, you'd still be too much of a player for me."

What did she want, a stinking saint who'd never kissed a woman? Asking her that question wasn't going to help his cause. "I understand you have a lot of questions and maybe doubts about me, and honestly, I have questions about you too. Can we just slow this down and give each other a chance? You've got to admit there's a spark between us."

Izzy stared at him, considering. Finally, she gave his hand a squeeze. "Does slowing it down mean no kissing?"

Xavier rubbed his thumb along the soft skin on the back of her hand. "Maybe for a few minutes."

Izzy glanced down at their joined hands then up at him. Sighing, she held onto his hand and tugged him toward the gate. "Let me beat you at paintball. Then we'll see about the rest."

Xavier laughed. He liked her far too much considering the baggage she came with.

7

Izzy had a fabulous time running around the huge paintball area, climbing onto towers and shooting people then ducking behind walls, only to peek out seconds later to try to take a pot shot. She'd never done this before, and it was a riot. In the first game, she and Xavier had been on separate teams, and her team had won. She had thought he would want a rematch, but for the second round, he made it so they were on the same team, which was truthfully so much more fun. They stayed close together, dodging, shooting, and laughing. She could almost put the memory of his lips on hers and his body surrounding her on the back burner. Almost.

They were running away from what seemed to be the entire opposing team when Izzy spotted a great spot for protection behind stacks of straw bales that formed a tall fort of sorts.

"X!" She yelled and pointed, sprinting that direction. The shots came sure and true. Xavier leapt in front of her to protect her from getting hit. He took several yellow paintballs in the back. Izzy dove, and he flew into the makeshift shelter after her, landing almost on top of her.

Izzy gasped for air from the run and his closeness.

"Guess I'm hit," he muttered. "Did they get you?"

"No, sir. You protected me well." She liked him being her protector, but she tilted her chin up at him and gave him a little sass instead of a kiss like she wanted to. "Guess I'm the winner again."

Xavier laughed, but then he sobered and leaned into her, pinning her against the wall of straw bales. "I love that you just called me, X."

"That isn't reserved for the Triple Threat?" Her breath was coming in fast pants, and her stomach filled up with butterflies.

He grinned. "The whole team actually calls me that ... and one beautiful princess."

SHE PUSHED AT HIS SHOULDER—HIS VERY NICELY FORMED SHOULDER. *Oh, Izzy, stop drooling.* "You can't call me princess. Look at me right now." She gestured around at what they'd been doing for the past couple of hours and then to her dirty, paint-splattered and muddy clothes. He grabbed her hand.

"You're right." His head lowered closer to hers, and she knew he was going to kiss her. She wanted it so badly, but she couldn't be moving this quick with him, becoming all comfortable and kissing nonstop. She was the no-nonsense nurse who didn't let men into her heart.

"Why *do* they call you X?" she asked, their breath intermingling, he was so close.

He lifted some hair away from her neck, brushing the sensitive skin with his fingertips. "If I tell you, it has to stay in this straw fort."

She smiled, so tempted to cross those inches and taste his incredible lips again. "I swear it."

"I trust you." He stared at her, and she felt like he really did trust her, but could she trust him? He'd sort of claimed he wasn't a womanizer, but wasn't that what every player said? She was sure when her father imported her mother from Columbia, he didn't say, *Hey, I'm going to be a cheating scumbag and have an affair with the beauty next door while you wither away from cancer.* She blinked away those horrible thoughts and focused on Xavier.

"So ... X?" It gave her a little thrill to call him that. Like they really were close friends.

"When I was in pee-wee league I was huge—off the growth charts in height and weight. It didn't help that I was hungry all the time, and my mama fed me nonstop. Supposedly, that's her 'love language.'" He winked. "The coaches didn't even give me a chance to play a skilled position and put an X on my helmet. I was stuck on the O-line until I hit high school."

"Wow. Look how quickly you picked up a skilled position."

Several warrior cries from above jerked them out of their comfortable conversation and cuddled position. Izzy looked up just as they were splattered with yellow paint. She took one to the cheek that stung, but she couldn't help but laugh along with Xavier. Several members of the other team had climbed the outside of the straw bale stack while they'd been distracted with each other.

"We surrender!" Izzy yelled.

"Speak for yourself," Xavier said, shooting several rounds at the young adults perched high above them. He shot one kid squarely in the chest with red paint and another took a hit to the arm.

"Hey, you can't shoot us after you get tagged out," a blonde girl protested.

"He's Xavier Newton. He can do whatever he wants."

The others laughed and agreed with that then started climbing down. Izzy realized she was impressed that up until that move Xavier had studiously followed the rules, and none of the other players had said anything about who he was.

"Did you have to pay the other players to be here?" she asked.

Xavier stood and offered her a hand up. "Yeah. It sucks to pay for friends, but these guys are professionals and agreed not to act like it was a big deal that I catch a football on Sundays. I didn't want to deal with people off the street freaking out, or invite my teammates and have them razz you nonstop." His voice lowered. "Or hit on you."

Once again, Izzy was overheated by a simple look from Xavier.

A young man came around the corner. "I know you only planned on two rounds, but we have time for one more round before we open to the public, sir. If you're interested."

Xavier looked to her.

"I'd love that," she said.

"Sounds great, Tyson. Thanks." Xavier gave Izzy a mischievous look. "But I think we'd better go boys against girls. You and I have to prove how tough we are, right bud?"

Tyson grinned from ear to ear. "Yes, sir!"

"Don't be salty when I beat you a third time." Izzy walked toward the staging area to get a different color of paint in her gun.

"Salty?" Xavier asked, hurrying to her side.

"Crying big old salty tears. I know how sensitive you are and all."

Xavier grinned. "I'll cry to my mama if you don't promise me at least one more kiss today."

"Your mama better be ready to comfort her big, old football player with lots of food. I already told you I don't kiss on the first date."

Xavier threw back his head and laughed.

———

XAVIER TURNED INTO A GATED COMMUNITY WITH MASSIVE HOMES, EACH with decent-sized lots and professional landscaping. Izzy had grown up in a Spanish mansion, the only thing about her mother's heritage that her father had retained, but this was still impressive. He drove into the circle drive of a Tudor-style mansion with large windows and ivy crawling all over the exterior. Izzy fell in love, but then the suspicions about Xavier's reputation reared their ugly head.

"Your house?" she asked tartly.

"Yes, ma'am." Xavier drummed his fingers on the steering wheel.

"Why did you bring me here?"

He turned to her with his brow furrowed. "So you could change your clothes before lunch."

Her jaw dropped, and she felt instant remorse.

"Why did you think I brought you here?"

"Well, you know, your reputation and all."

He nodded shortly, jumped out, and jogged around to get her door. "Princess."

The way he said it, so short and tight, made her fight to keep her composure. She stepped down from the Land Rover, clutching the bag with her change of clothes. Xavier gestured her toward the front steps, flanked with green shrubs and the deep purple flowers she knew as Texas stars. "Your home is beautiful. I'm sorry for assuming the worst."

He studied her for a few seconds before pushing out a long breath. "It seems like I've got a long road to getting you to trust me."

Izzy folded her arms across her chest and focused on the green Texas ash trees blocking the view of the neighbor's home. "Honestly, it's not all you, X."

Her using his nickname brought a small smile to his face. "What do you mean?"

"My father may have ruined me from ever fully trusting a man."

Xavier's mouth went slack. "Was he a cheater?"

She nodded, not ready to have this conversation standing on the driveway. Okay, she might never be ready to have this conversation.

Xavier took the bag from her hand and then offered his other hand. Izzy glanced down at his dark brown fingers then back up into his beautiful eyes. Finally, she took his hand. He walked slowly across the cement and up the stairs, releasing her hand to punch in a code, swing the front door wide, and gesture her inside. Izzy loved him a little bit at that moment for not trying to force the details out of her.

She walked into the exquisite two-story foyer, lit by all the windows. There were fresh flowers on the entry table and perfectly placed landscape paintings and mirrors on the sea foam walls. She loved the contrast to the rich cherry wood trim and woodwork. Xavier took her hand again and led her to the stairs. An unfamiliar feeling washed over her, like she could fight through anything with her hand in his and this strong man by her side.

The wide staircase led to a double-sided balcony that looked down on the foyer and formal office and dining room on the front side and the great room and kitchen on the back. The two-story windows from the front and rear of the house brought in plenty of the bright Texas sun. Xavier still hadn't said anything. They walked along the walkway to the right-hand side where several doors were lined up. She assumed it was the space above the garage. He released her hand and pushed open one of the doors, but stopped on the threshold.

"This is the room my mama stays in when she comes and visits, so there's plenty of girlie shampoo and lotion if you want to use them."

"Thank you." Izzy dipped her head, thinking how horribly she'd misjudged him again. He hadn't tried to come into the bedroom with her, and he wasn't going to try to stain her virtue in the room his mama stayed in.

"Izzy," he whispered her name, and she met his gaze again. "I'm sorry your father hurt you and your mama, but there are many men who stay true when they make a promise."

Izzy held his gaze. He believed what he was telling her. Could she ever believe such a thing? Leave the past in the past and trust in a man? She'd fought her way through school and worked hard to succeed in her career. Now, she had the freedom to help children and the hospital, and she was respected by her peers and loved by the children. How would a man fit into her structured life?

He nodded to her then turned and walked away. Izzy watched him go before quietly shutting the door and carrying her bag into the attached bathroom. She smiled wryly as she caught a glimpse of herself in the gilded mirror—yellow, red, and blue paint stained her face and clothes, and hair. Xavier had treated her like a lady, no matter how many times she misjudged him and how horrible she looked. She opened the glass door of the shower, stepped into the granite interior, and pulled the knob to warm up the water before shedding her dirty clothes. Xavier had definitely given her plenty to think about.

———

XAVIER SHOWERED IN HIS MASTER SUITE THAT WAS SITUATED ON THE opposite side of the kitchen and garage next to the great room, having to scrub hard at some of the paint splatters. After drying off, he put on a clean pair of gray shorts and a faded blue short-sleeved button-down shirt. Izzy had him so stirred up and confused. He wished he could call his mama for advice. He walked out into the great room, grasping his phone, but not wanting to get caught spilling his guts to her if Izzy came out.

He glanced up at the open balcony, willing Izzy to appear. He wanted to talk through so many things with her, but the hurt in her eyes when she revealed what her father was like told him to take it slow. She'd placed trust in him revealing her family secret, and he didn't want to mess it up by rushing her.

He turned his focus to the floor-to-ceiling two-story windows and his landscaped backyard. The trees, bushes, and fence gave him lots of privacy. He really enjoyed his home, but it often felt too perfect to him—professionally decorated, cleaned, and landscaped. What this place really needed was a couple of little boys to throw things off the balcony, ding the walls racing each other on their scooters, and shoot Nerf bullets all over the place. And maybe a little princess to keep the boys in line, even though she'd be every bit as tough as they were. He was kind of liking princesses right now.

His front door popped open. Dang it, giving Kade his security code was a mistake. He'd need to change it again.

"X?" Kade called out, stomping his way through the entry, around the staircase, and into the great room. "Oh, good, you're home."

"What were you going to do if I wasn't home?"

"Steal some of the cookies Mama left for me in the freezer."

Xavier shook his head. Mama always stocked his freezer with meals and treats before she left, and Ace and Kade knew the food was for them as much as for Xavier.

"Help yourself."

"I always do." Kade walked into the pantry, which was as big as most people's kitchens. Xavier could hear him swing open the industrial-sized freezer and rummage around. Then the microwave turned on for a brief time. He came back out with a plate stacked with choco-late chip cookies. Xavier studied his friend. His normally cocksure expression was gone, and although Xavier knew Kade loved Mama's cookies, he was pretty diligent about eating only a few and not consuming too much sugar and carbs. They were professional athletes after all.

"Everything okay?" Xavier asked.

"This woman has got me off my game, man." He got himself a glass of milk from the fridge then sat down at the seven-foot granite bar and started dunking cookies.

Xavier sat down a few stools over. He wanted to help his friend, but Izzy was going to be coming out of that upstairs bedroom door any minute, and he didn't want Kade teasing him or Izzy getting embarrassed by being caught coming out of one of his bedrooms.

"You think I've got advice about women?" Xavier asked.

"Of course you do. You date a different hot girl every other day."

Xavier's neck heated up. Even though he'd tried to explain to his closest friends what a fraud his dating life was, they didn't really understand it. "What's her name?" He felt compelled to ask.

"Felicity Song." Kade shoved half a cookie in.

"Felicity Song?" Xavier repeated. "The redhead from the auction?"

"Yeah. You know she bought the date with me, but she doesn't want—"

The door swung open upstairs, and then soft footsteps padded across the balcony and down the staircase.

Kade froze with a cookie halfway to his mouth. His eyes widened as he looked at Xavier then looked to the arched opening where Izzy appeared. She looked unreal beautiful in a simple white sundress that showcased her tanned and firm shoulders. Her dark hair was still wet, and her wide eyes darted between him and Kade.

"Oh, hey, I didn't know ..." He grinned at Xavier. "Going for the owner's daughter. Mad respect for your game, my friend."

Izzy blinked at him, and Xavier shook his head. How to clear this up? Kade obviously thought they had ... and he didn't want Izzy thinking that he was like that with women, but she probably would. Oh, sheesh.

Kade picked up his plate of cookies, set his glass of milk in the sink, and saluted Xavier with the cookies. "I'll bring the plate back." His eyes swung to Izzy again, and he muttered, "Mad respect." He walked toward her and extended his hand. "Kade Kincaid. Nice to meet you, Miss Knight."

She shook his hand. "You as well."

"Keep this guy in line, will you?"

Izzy tossed her long, dark hair and folded her arms under her chest. "No, thank you. Not applying for that job."

Kade regarded her for a second. "Your loss. There are plenty that are."

Xavier loved that his friend felt like he needed to step up for him, but it was the worst thing he could say to Izzy with her insecurities.

"I'm fully aware of that, Kade Kincaid."

Kade arched his eyebrows. "Well, that's my cue to leave." He glanced back at Xavier. "Forget about *my* woman trouble." He inclined his chin and was gone. The implication was loud and clear —Xavier's woman trouble was much worse than whatever Kade had wanted to chat about. Maybe, but at least Xavier wasn't downing a dozen cookies.

Izzy hadn't moved from the entryway into the great room.

"Ah," Xavier said. "He didn't really mean—"

"Where are we going to lunch?" Izzy asked, all crisp and formal.

Xavier wanted to hang his head. This was never going to work. Any time he broke through her barriers, which were stronger than concrete, something happened to build them back up, the next time with reinforced rebar. He wondered if it was even worth it to try to hammer them down again.

"You're going to love it," he said, forcing an unconcerned grin. "You know Ace Sanchez?"

"Heard of him." She offered him a tentative smile. She probably wasn't anxious to meet another teammate after the exchange with Kade.

"His family owns one of the best Mexican restaurants in the Metroplex."

"That's a big claim." She arched an eyebrow and everything from her beautiful face to the challenge in her eyes was really appealing to him. Could he kiss her again? No, probably not good timing.

"If I'm wrong, you get to choose where we go to dinner." At least, he could try to spend a little more time with her.

"You think I'm spending the entire day with you?" She tucked her long hair behind her ear.

Xavier flicked his thumb against his leg. He wanted to spend the entire day with her. Although he'd planned to knock her off her princess pedestal and take her to the demolition derby tonight and buy her a greasy hamburger or corndog, he'd put on a three-piece suit and take her to The Mansion Restaurant with their signature over a hundred dollar-a-plate meals if she wanted that. But he wouldn't force her to stay with him, and he wasn't getting the best vibe from her right now.

"I would like that." His voice went all husky on him, and he cursed himself for being such a sap.

She blinked at him a couple of times, those long eyelashes fanning against her cheek. She wore feminine-tough better than any woman he'd met with her fit body, smart mind, and successful career, yet she was still so soft and exquisitely beautiful.

"We'll see." She said it flirtatiously and even flipped her hair.

Xavier smiled, knowing his dimples were showing and hoping she really did love them like she had said when she'd kissed him before paintball. Maybe this date could be salvaged after all, and getting to know Izzy better was still his most important objective.

8

They walked into the restaurant, Los Tios, near the historical section of Fort Worth with Xavier's hand on the small of her back. Izzy's cheeks were flushed, and her mind was whirling with the conflicting evidence she kept being handed about Xavier. Kade Kincaid had basically confirmed Xavier was a player, but Xavier had said he was someone she could trust. She wanted to trust him, and she really wanted him to keep touching her and this date to never end, but reality had to come into play, and she worried it was going to hit her hard.

The restaurant had bright yellow walls with sombreros and blankets hanging on them. The red booths and black tables provided an attractive contrast. Izzy was happy he'd brought her here. She adored Mexican food and felt an immediate connection to the bright, warm spot. Her mother would've loved it. The restaurant was crowded, but the young Spanish greeter immediately recognized Xavier.

"X!" He hollered.

Many patrons turned, and then it seemed like the entire restaurant was staring at them. A few teenage girls pulled out their phones and snapped pictures. Xavier released his hold on her and grasped the hand the young man offered, clapping him on the shoulder. "Antonio, what is this? You're going to be bigger than me soon."

The wiry teenager poked out his chest. "I'm already taller than my parents. I'll pass Ace up by next year."

"For sure! Great to see you, my friend."

"You want a private table?" He winked at Izzy, and she couldn't help but like him. It wasn't a lewd wink, more friendly and innocent. She judged he was about seventeen and loved his smile. It reminded her of Ace Sanchez. She hadn't formally met Ace, but he seemed like a great guy.

Xavier's hand went to her back again, and Izzy couldn't help but love it there.

"Izzy, this is Antonio, Ace's little brother."

"Not little for long. Nice to meet you, Izzy." He stuck out his hand and shook hers. Izzy liked that his parents had taught him old-fashioned manners. He grabbed two sets of cloth-wrapped utensils and menus and hurried in front of them. "Follow me, my friends. I'll find you a good table then let Ace and Mom know you're here."

"No Dad today?"

"He'll be in soon. He's unclogging the bathroom drain. Ace told him to call a plumber, but you know how he is."

They threaded through tables as Antonio talked. Everyone seemed to be staring at them and whispers of "That's Xavier Newton" were everywhere. Izzy knew it would be like this because she'd grown up around professional athletes, what with her father owning the team, but it was still unnerving to her. Did she really want to be dating someone who would always throw her in the public limelight? She scoffed at herself. It was only one date.

"My mama is the same way," Xavier was saying. "She'll spend hours gluing a glass back together when I'm begging her to go buy a new one."

Antonio laughed. "Same generation. Good people though, right?" He gestured toward a corner booth where they would have a decent amount of privacy. "This all right?"

"Perfect." Xavier waited while Izzy slid onto the vinyl bench then sat across from her. Izzy would've liked to stay close to him, but this was better. They could face each other and talk. Somehow it felt too intimate to sit side by side. Even though they'd kissed, they weren't a couple, and she needed to remember that.

Antonio set their menus down and smiled at Izzy. "Have you been here before?"

"Sorry to say I haven't."

"Best Mexican food in Ft. Worth," Antonio said proudly.

Xavier grinned cockily, and Izzy wanted to touch his dimples.

"Everybody will tell you to get the tamales but take it from me, beef chimichanga is the ticket. You'll thank me." He kind of clucked his tongue and nodded.

"Beef chimichanga, got it."

He winked again. "I'll go let them know you're here."

Xavier didn't open his menu but studied her. "I didn't think about this being a little overwhelming for you."

"All the fans watching us?"

His eyes widened, and he glanced out at the crowded restaurant where most of the patrons were still staring at him. "Oh, um, no. Sorry, I'm so used to that I didn't even think of it."

Interesting. She supposed you would have to get used to constant scrutiny and awed looks if you were playing at Xavier's level, but it made her feel like a fish in a tank. Amazingly, no one had approached them yet.

"I meant all the attention from Ace's family," he said.

"Antonio was great."

"He is, but just you wait."

The kitchen doors burst open, and a pretty woman with short, curly hair and black eyes rushed to their table and exclaimed, "Hola, my hijo!"

Xavier stood and wrapped her in his arms. She was probably about five five but looked teeny next to Xavier. He released her and smiled down at her. She clapped a hand on either side of his face. "Those dimples! How does anyone resist them?" She turned and arched an eyebrow at Izzy. "Am I right?"

"Unfortunately," Izzy said then realized that probably wasn't the positive response this lady was looking for. "Yes, you're right, ma'am."

"Mama Fabiana," Xavier said. "This is Izzy Knight."

"Nice to meet you, love." Fabiana extended her hand. Izzy stood, and they shook quickly. "I hope you're treating mi hijo something special. He deserves a princess."

Izzy couldn't contain the too-loud laugh that sputtered out. Fabiana looked offended. Xavier saved her. "I call her princess all the time."

"Oh, I see." She pinned Izzy with a look. "And are you treating him like royalty?"

Izzy didn't know how to respond, so she opted for the truth. "Not usually."

"Well, you see that you do." She inclined her chin at Izzy, but a light sparkled mischievously in those dark eyes. "I'll send Ace out." She focused on Izzy again. "Try the tamales. They're my specialty." She kissed her fingers, waved them at Xavier and was gone.

Xavier waited for Izzy to sit back down then sank back into his side of the bench.

"I don't think I impressed her," Izzy said, really wishing she had. She seemed like a warm, loving woman.

"Ah, she's just a little overprotective of me. That's all."

"Yes, you definitely need someone protecting you."

Xavier laughed.

The chatter in the restaurant seemed to have resumed, and Izzy didn't feel like everyone was staring at them quite as much. That was, until the kitchen door opened again, and Ace Sanchez strode out. He was an extremely handsome man with smooth, brown skin, a fit body, and a smile that had been plastered all over Texas, probably all over the nation.

Xavier saw him and stood, and they embraced. Izzy heard phones clicking throughout the restaurant. She stood, and Ace turned to her, grinning. "So nice to meet you, Izzy."

"You as well." She shook the hand he offered and tried to ignore all the pictures being taken of the exchange. When the media figured out that she and Xavier had gone on their million-dollar date it was going to get insane. The charity banquet had only allowed one professional photographer in the other night, and so except for entering and exiting, the paparazzi hadn't had much material to go on.

Ace released her hand and inclined his chin to Xavier. "Good luck with this monstrosity. He doesn't know how to behave."

"Hey!" Xavier cried out. "And here Mama Fabiana was telling her to treat me like royalty."

"Chh." Ace made a dismissive sound with his tongue. "She hasn't had to deal with you on the field."

"Hey, just because my calves and biceps are more defined than yours is no reason to get salty with me." Xavier winked at her, and she loved that he'd stolen her word.

"Salty?" Ace's brow wrinkled.

"Crying big salty tears."

Ace threw back his head and laughed. "I'd tell Mom to hold me while I cried if *The Rising Star* hadn't just done an article and claimed my calves were the most perfect in the NFL."

"Liar." Xavier shook his head but was chuckling. "*The Rising Star* has a bunch of idiot reporters."

"For sure." Ace agreed. "They keep putting you on their Most Handsome Men list. Raving lunatics."

Izzy smiled at the interchange. "You two always tease each other?"

"Pretty much." Xavier nodded. "It's our MO."

"Hey, I've got to go cook tortillas until my dad gets here. He's off unclogging a bathroom drain." Ace shook his head and folded his arms across his chest. He wasn't exaggerating about his biceps. They were impressive, but not quite as impressive as Xavier's, at least not to her. "I keep begging them to hire more help, but they want it to stay 'family run' and all that."

"You'd probably have less of a crowd if they didn't know they might catch a glimpse of you on a Saturday," Izzy said to Ace.

Ace quirked an eyebrow. "Good point. Everybody wants a peep at these biceps." He flexed.

Izzy loved that he was teasing. Of course, these guys were confident, but she could tell they weren't really that into themselves. Ace glanced out the restaurant door where a line was forming. He inclined his chin toward it. "That's my cue to disappear. Good luck, X."

"We'll just hide here in our little booth."

"Yeah, that'll work." Ace gave them a jaunty wave and hurried back to the kitchen.

Xavier and Izzy sank into the booth again, and Izzy really wished she could hide behind something. She glanced out at the crowded restaurant and the serious line now forming out on the sidewalk.

"Do you think people posted that you and Ace were both here and it spread that quickly?"

"I wouldn't put anything past social media. Sorry. You okay staying?"

If her father had wanted publicity out of her date with Xavier, he was going to get it. She wanted to run and hide, but she took a breath and pasted on a brave face "Of course. I have to try the chimichangas."

Xavier favored her with his dimpled smile. A petite twenty-something waitress with gorgeous black hair approached their table with a tray and set down big glasses of ice water, straws, a basket of chips, and a large bowl of salsa. "Hi, X." She greeted him casually, as if he was no big deal. "The usual?"

"Yes, ma'am."

She gave him a smile and a nod. She noticed Izzy's closed menu. "Would you like some recommendations?"

"No, Antonio said I have to try the beef chimichangas."

"He would," she said dryly. "Refried or black beans?"

"Black, please."

"Sour cream and guacamole okay?"

"Wouldn't miss them."

She smiled. "Gotcha." She put her pad back in her pocket and rushed away.

Izzy dipped a still-warm chip into the salsa, scooping up a big bite and putting it all in her mouth.

"Careful, that's—" Xavier started.

"Hot!" Izzy managed to say around the bite. Her tongue was on fire and sweat broke out on her upper lip. She grabbed her glass of ice water and sucked half of it down.

Xavier chuckled.

Izzy swallowed and then drank some more water to try to soothe her tongue. "But delicious," she said, going for another chip but not taking quite as much salsa.

"For sure."

She couldn't resist sneaking another glance at the crowds of people, each seeming to either be craning their necks for a peek at Xavier Newton or watching the kitchen door hoping Ace Sanchez would walk back out.

"Does it get old?" she asked, breaking a chip in half but not eating it.

Xavier nodded. "At Air Force, they tried pretty hard to not make us feel special."

"Why'd you choose Air Force?" He could've played college ball anywhere.

"Close to home, good athletics program, best scholarship offer I had." He dunked a chip and plunged it into his mouth. "It delayed me playing professionally a little bit since I was on active duty two years before I committed to the Titans."

She imagined he would've been great in the military, but she couldn't conceive of a world where he wouldn't have been snatched up by a smart recruiter. He was one of the best players in the nation. "Are you in the reserves now?"

He nodded.

She hadn't known that about him, but it fit. He was disciplined and hard-working and suddenly she was having all kinds of visions of him in an Air Force uniform. She fanned her face. Was it hot in here? "The salsa," she murmured, clasping her hands together in her lap.

"Where did you go to school?" Xavier asked.

"Texas A&M." She suddenly felt the pressure and stress again throughout high school and college. She'd worked hard. "When they offered me a tuition scholarship, I cried. I can't imagine how great a full-ride offer would be."

He tilted his head to study her. "I hope this isn't offensive because you shared with me why you don't respect your dad, but he has to be a multi-billionaire. Why did you need a scholarship?"

She looked down at the black tabletop then reluctantly met his eyes. "I hate my father, and when I turned eighteen, I moved out and refused to take a cent from him."

His eyes widened. "Wow, that's impressive." He looked her over, and it seemed like he was seeing her in a new light. "Is that why you don't want me calling you princess?"

She ate a fragment of chip, liking the light grease and thin texture. "I don't mind it so much from you."

The waitress returned with two drinks. "Mango lemonade for X, and I apologize, but I forgot to ask what you wanted to drink, ma'am. I brought a strawberry lemonade, but we have Coke products, Budweiser, or I can bring the wine list."

"This is great." Izzy reassured her, not telling her that she rarely drank anything besides water. Her little sister, Hailey, loved to tease her about how boring she was. She stirred the drink and took a small sip, pleasing the waitress who rushed off again. It was a nice mix of sweet strawberry syrup and tart lemonade and soothed her mouth that was sweltering from the delicious salsa and her dreams of Xavier in an Air Force uniform.

Xavier was staring intently at her. "If you don't take money from your father, how did you buy me for a million dollars?"

Izzy's neck and cheeks went hot, and she couldn't blame it on the jalapenos much longer. "He knows how to manipulate me, and the children's hospital is my life now. So many families can't afford their treatments, even with insurance or governmental help. Then there's the research for things like juvenile diabetes, cancer, AIDS, and so many diseases that need more funding all the time. We have to find cures someday." If only they could've had a cure for her mother. She splayed her hands wide and tried to tease. "Do you think I sold out?"

Xavier slowly shook his head. "No. I'm trying to recalculate everything in my brain. I wasn't sure why Knight would have you buy me and then double the bid. He must care about you a lot."

Izzy felt a rush of familial love that she quickly extinguished. She remembered many years ago when she'd had a daddy who she'd run to when he came home from work. He'd pick her up and hug her. Now, she barely acknowledged she had a father. If it wasn't for Dolly and Hailey, she would never have any contact with the man.

"No." She squeaked out and quickly took another pull of her lemonade, wishing that she did drink something stronger. "You said your mama's love language was food, well my father's is money." Yet sometimes, she wondered during the few times she saw him interact with Dolly and Hailey, who were obviously both very happy and very much in love with the man. Izzy would never call her stepmom or half-sister shallow because she adored them, but money seemed to be their love language too. Maybe that's why it all worked for them, and Izzy was left out of the circle. By choice, but left out all the same.

"I'm sorry," he said simply.

"It's life, families. So let's go back to how you deal with the constant fans." She peeked out at the restaurant crowd again, and though most of the patrons inside were eating and seemed distracted, the line outside was long and intimidating.

Xavier studied her like he wasn't ready to change subject, but he was gracious enough to not force it. He lifted his broad shoulders. "At first, I ate it up. I'd gotten attention in high school and college, then while I was in the military I was definitely nothing special." He grinned. "Nothing could've prepared me for that first year in the pros. But it gets old pretty quick, and you find yourself just ignoring people, which isn't cool, but sometimes, you have no choice if you're going to ever get someplace on time. I can't ever walk away from the kiddos though."

"You were very kind to Tyson at the paintball place." She hadn't missed the fact that Xavier had slipped him a roll of twenties and told him to share it with his friends. She liked that a lot.

"Nice kid. They were all great to not make a big fuss about me."

"You're kind of fun to make a fuss about."

Xavier's eyes sparkled at her, and his hand reached across the table toward hers. Unfortunately, at that moment, their waitress arrived with steaming plates of food. She set them down in front of each of them and nudged them closer with her hot-pad hands. "Be careful, plates are hot. Can I get you anything else?" With narrowed eyes, she stared at their basket of chips, which was still piled high, as if they were jerks to not devour it.

Xavier looked to Izzy.

She shook her head and said, "This looks great."

He nodded. "Thank you."

She took off again.

"She's in a hurry." Izzy remarked, picking up her fork and cutting a steaming bite.

"Ace is always saying they need to hire more staff. A lot of times, you'll see Mama Fabiana bussing the dining room floor or one of Ace's brothers or cousins. They all work really hard."

Izzy blew on the bite and then finally placed it in her mouth. Cheesy goodness rested there. The meat was tender steak, the rice and beans were perfectly seasoned, and the homemade tortilla and guacamole blended flawlessly. She chewed slowly, savoring it before saying, "Best Mexican food I've ever tasted."

"Aw, yeah." Xavier drawled it out, pointing his fork at her before cutting a bite of his tamale. "That means I get to choose dinner too."

"You're really planning on me being around for dinner?" Izzy teased. She'd been concerned at his house with the obvious implications from his teammate, Kade, that Xavier was a womanizer. She'd known that fact going into the date, but she still didn't know how to resist him. Her mouth turned down. That was probably what every other woman felt.

"I really hope you will be." He glanced down as if suddenly shy. She knew that couldn't be true, but it felt like it. He met her gaze again, his dark eyes beseeching. "So far this has been the best date of my life."

She got lost in the dark depths of his eyes, her fork clattering to the plate. "You mean the best first date?"

"No." He shook his head. "I mean best date."

"I still don't kiss on the first date." She insisted, wanting to flirt with him.

"So those first two kisses?" His voice went low and sultry, and she wasn't hungry for the best Mexican food anymore.

"You kissed me." She reminded him, but that wasn't exactly true. There'd been a third kiss that she'd instigated, right after she'd cupped his face and told him how she loved his dimples. Oh, my, this food was really spicy. She took another gulp of water.

"Oh, so that's how you work? As long as I initiate, I can plan on more of that bit of heaven?"

Dang he was smooth. She laughed. "You've got me. But you're going to have to work hard for the next kiss."

"I've had to work hard a few times in my life."

Izzy smiled at the understatement. He could write a book on rising from the ashes through hard work.

"This work sounds like a lot of fun." He winked and went back to his tamales and tostada lunch.

Izzy had a hard time focusing on cutting another bite of chimichanga as she imagined kissing him again. It wouldn't be work for her, not at all. This date was not turning out to be anything like she'd thought it would, and she might give into another kiss … or two.

9

Xavier wrapped his arm around Izzy to escort her out of the restaurant, dropping a hundred-dollar bill on the table because Mama Fabiana refused to let him pay the bill. There was still a huge line out front, and people kept edging closer and closer to him and Izzy. He kept a smile plastered on his face but hurried Izzy toward the door. Hopefully, they could escape without being mauled. Mama Fabiana had offered the kitchen exit, but his Land Rover was out front, so he'd have to get through the crowd somehow.

Nobody tried to bar their path, but Izzy was tense against his side. People in Texas knew who she was too, and there were a lot of pictures getting snapped right now. They said goodbye to Antonio and cleared the door, and a buzz went up in the crowd. Xavier had learned to not engage if he needed to get through and he didn't want Izzy to have to deal with the questions and harassment if the crowd got out of control.

He bent down closer to her. "Just keep walking. They're good people, just excited to see someone famous."

"I'm okay, X." She smiled up at him, and he fell a little harder for her. She was made of much tougher stuff than anyone would guess. Most of the girls he dated loved the attention of crowds. Izzy wasn't into it, but she wasn't falling apart because people were making a fuss over them.

"Xavier! Mr. Newton!" The cries came from less than twenty feet away. It didn't sound like a typical fan, it sounded like paparazzi. He glanced up and sure enough, several high-dollar cameras started snapping. "Are you and Ms. Knight dating? How does her father feel about this?" One of them called out, goading.

Xavier kept walking, upping his pace. A tug on his right arm made him tense up. He shielded Izzy with his body while preparing to duke it out to protect her. This was not going to go over well with his agent.

"Mr. Newton?" an innocent voice queried.

Xavier glanced down. A little boy of about ten or eleven, thick-waisted with red hair and a big smile, looked worshipfully up at him. "Would you mind signing my football, sir?"

Xavier stopped and glanced at Izzy. She gave him an encouraging smile. Luckily, the paparazzi held back and stopped yelling questions at them. "For sure, bud, what's your name?"

"Luke."

He took the football and the pen. It was a regular pen, not a permanent marker which made it a little more difficult, but he did his standard. *To Luke. Word hard. Pray hard. Xavier Newton.* He handed it back and couldn't resist ruffling the kid's hair. "Be good for your, Mama, you hear?"

The crowd sighed.

Luke nodded, and the boy's blonde mother beamed next to him. "Sir, is it true you were a X-head in peewees?"

"And proud of it." Xavier chuckled and looked the kid over. "You an X?"

"Yeah."

"Keep doing your best, and you'll find your spot."

The kid broke into another wide grin. "Thank you, sir."

Xavier grinned at him, but could feel the crowd pressing closer. He bent down and whispered, "You want to distract them while I get my girl out of here?"

Luke glanced at Izzy and let out a low, appreciative whistle. "I got it, sir."

Xavier held out his fist, and Luke bumped it. Xavier started directing Izzy toward the Land Rover and Luke hollered louder than Xavier would've thought a boy could yell, "Look, Mom! Look! Ace Sanchez and Kade Kincaid! This is my best day ever!"

Xavier was tempted to look himself, but instead, he pulled Izzy toward his vehicle, unlocking it, and ripping her door open while the paparazzi and crowd turned to catch a glimpse of Ace and Kade. She leapt inside, and he shut the door and rushed around to his side. He pulled out onto the road before he glanced back. The crowd was still searching for Ace and Kade, but Luke was giving him a big grin and a thumb's up.

Xavier drove off, laughing. "I hope I have a kid like that someday."

Izzy pushed her seatbelt into place. "He was adorable. Thanks for being so great with him."

"I thought we were going to get mauled by that crowd, but I couldn't leave my little man hanging."

"Were Ace and Kade really there?"

"Naw. I told my buddy to distract the crowd so I could get my girl to safety."

"If only I was actually your girl." There was a teasing lilt to her voice.

"If only." He reached across the console and squeezed her hand.

"So what else do you have planned for our grand adventure?" Izzy asked, holding onto his hand, which he really liked.

"Well, I'd planned on giving the princess a few redneck experiences—paintball, demolition derby, and the fair. But we can do anything you want. We could go back to my place and swim or take my boat out on Lake Lewisville." He held his breath. Rejection hadn't happened to him in a long while, but he was fully prepared for it at this moment.

"I don't know that I want to repeat the restaurant experience anytime soon, so sadly, the demolition derby might be out."

"You think a bunch of rednecks would recognize a football player?"

She laughed. "The only thing worse would be if you raced NASCAR."

"True."

"Boating sounds fun," she said. "I haven't been out on a lake in years."

"Great." He looked over at her. "You don't let yourself have much leisure time, do you?"

"Too busy." She tucked her hair behind her ear.

"That is exactly my point. You're too busy for fun?"

"I'm sure you're busy too."

He shrugged. "During the season it's insane, but off-season, I have a little more free time. Time to take a beautiful princess out boating."

"I used to think you were making fun of me with the princess thing, but I'm not so sure anymore."

Xavier squeezed her hand. "You're a very impressive lady. I wouldn't dream of making fun of you."

10

Izzy didn't know what to plan on with Xavier's boat or with Xavier for that matter, but she loved his Malibu Wakesetter with the deep red exterior and gray faux-leather seats and carpet inside. He must've placed a call to have the boat ready while she was at her condo getting her swimsuit and cover-up because the boat was in the lake, all ready to go when they arrived. They walked down the dock, and Xavier palmed the guy holding the boat steady some money. They climbed in quickly and were off.

Xavier sat in the driver's seat, and she perched on the cushion next to him. He put the boat into gear, and they skimmed along the water a few hundred yards before Xavier cut the motor. He stood and walked to the rear of the boat.

"You're up first," he said, grinning at her then opening a padded compartment on the back of the boat and pulling out a pink life-jacket. "Hopefully, this'll fit. I only have one female jacket."

Izzy lifted off her cover-up and took the jacket from him. His eyes brushed over her one-piece suit appreciatively, but he quickly refocused on her face. She felt pretty and daring in the high-necked floral suit that showed off a strip of her abdomen and made her legs look long and lean. Hailey had given it to her, and she was grateful for her sister's ability to shop.

She zipped and snapped the lifejacket on. "First for what?"

She glanced around at the busy lake. Everybody was looking to escape the muggy June heat. There were sailboats, ski boats, and surfing boats. It all looked fun, but she didn't have much experience at any of it and was a little bit nervous.

"Whatever you want to do—ski, wakeboard, surf, kneeboard, go barefoot." He winked.

"Oh, I'm definitely going for the barefoot." She kept a straight face for half a second.

He chuckled. "As tough as you are, you probably could."

Izzy flushed from the compliment. She'd fought hard to prove how tough she was, not needing help from anybody, and appreciated that he noticed that about her. "Honestly, I have never tried any of it. What's the easiest thing to learn?"

He cocked his head to the side. "That surprises me. Didn't you grow up here in Dallas?"

"Yes."

"And you've never been out on the lake?"

"Some friends brought me out a few times, but the boat was always crowded, and nobody noticed that I didn't do anything." Her father owned multiple boats and wave runners, but she'd always refused to go out with him. Apparently, Xavier had caught enough clues about that situation and wasn't going to ask.

"Well, today's the day for you to try it all out. Hmm." He pursed his lips. "Surfing is definitely the easiest thing to learn, and I think you'll like it."

"I have gone surfing before. My father got me and Hailey lessons in Hawaii a couple of times."

"See, this will be easy." He brushed past her and stepped up onto the side of the boat, lifting a board off the shiny silver rack that stuck out on either side of the shade cover thing. The board was only about half as long as a normal surfboard.

Walking past her again, Xavier set the board on the padded rear of the boat then lifted one of the seats opposite to where she was sitting and pulled out a short rope.

Izzy really enjoyed watching him in his gray plaid swimsuit and white neoprene shirt. He moved well. She smiled to herself. Big surprise that a professional athlete had fluid and attractive movements.

He attached the rope to a silver knob up high, behind the shade covering then motioned to her. "Okay. You'll be great at this."

Izzy stood and walked to him. He took her hand and helped her up over the padded rear of the boat onto a lower wooden platform that the water lapped over. He released her hand, sat down on the padded part and patted the spot next to him. "Right here."

"Bossy, bossy."

He flashed her his grin, and she wondered if those dimples would ever stop affecting her. It was probably ninety degrees with seventy percent humidity, but she was sweating from something completely different than the heat. Jumping in the water would be fabulous.

He lifted the board down onto the wooden platform and set his feet on it. "You just lay back in the water with your feet resting on the board and the rope held between your feet." He pantomimed holding a rope. "Let the boat pull you up and simply put pressure on your heels and then keep putting pressure on the board. You'll pop right up. Honestly, just hold onto the rope, and I'll do the rest. Easy."

"Easy." She repeated skeptically. It didn't sound easy at all. On a real surfboard, you jumped up and there was none of this business about something pulling you up and pressure on your heels.

"That's right." He handed her the rope and the board.

Izzy slid into the warm water and maneuvered around to face the boat while still holding onto the rope. It was so short she was only a couple of feet behind the rear platform of the boat. She rested her heels on the board like he'd told her and held onto the rope. Xavier went back to the driver's seat but stayed standing. He put the motor into gear, and it slowly puttered forward until the rope was taut. Then he pulled it back into neutral. She couldn't believe how quiet his boat's motor was. She supposed when you paid enough money, they figured out how to have the motor purr.

"You ready?" He called back.

"As I'll ever be."

He laughed and pushed the throttle forward. The board slid out from under her feet as she clung onto the rope. She flipped over onto her stomach and gulped in mouthfuls of lake water. The boat stopped, and she bobbed to a stop, still clinging to the rope. Blinking water out of her eyes, she looked up into Xavier's very concerned face. He must've rushed quickly from the driver's seat.

"Are you okay?"

She spit and wiped at her face. "Yeah, just a little waterlogged."

"What happened?"

"I wish I knew."

"Um, okay. First thing, don't hold onto the rope if you lose the board."

"Lesson learned." She couldn't help but spit again.

He laughed. "Second thing, as soon as you hear the boat engage you need to press down hard with your heels. I think what happened was the board stayed flat and just slid away from you. If you press with your heels, you get it on an angle, and then the boat will easily pull you up."

"Okay, first thing, you're making me try this again?"

"It's the rule of the lake that you have to try three times. You got this. It's easy."

"Okay, second thing, stop saying it's easy, or I'm going to slap you again."

Xavier chuckled and rubbed at his jaw. "I forgot you slapped me. That was kind of fun."

Her eyes widened.

"Okay, not the slap, but what happened before and what happened after."

Her face was burning despite the water surrounding her. "Must be too long of a date if you already forgot what happened this morning."

Xavier's deep brown eyes penetrated through her. "I didn't forget the kissing, not by any means."

He was either the smoothest ladies' man she'd ever met or he was really into her. Izzy wasn't sure which, and she forced herself to not comment and to look away from his gaze. She saw the board floating close by. She let go of the rope and swam over, bringing the board back and getting into position again. "Okay, I'm ready."

Xavier chuckled. "We'll focus on the kissing again after you surf."

Izzy shook her head and clung to the rope. Why he'd want to kiss her when she looked like a drowned rat was beyond her, but she couldn't put the kisses they shared out of her mind either.

"Okay, go now," she said.

"We usually say hit it." He smirked at her and put the boat into gear, taking the slack out of the line.

Izzy felt the tension on the rope and the board and yelled. "Hit it!"

Xavier shoved the boat into gear, and she pushed down hard with her heels. She easily stood up on the board and was so surprised she almost let go of the rope.

"Yes!" Xavier pumped his fist in the air. "Now keep a little more pressure on your back foot." He called to her.

As he said that, she felt the tip of her board plunging dangerously into the water. She pressed back, and it leveled out. The wake on his boat was massive, and after a few minutes of gliding along behind it, she got brave and started turning the board into the wake and out of it.

"You're doing great!" Xavier hollered, alternating between glancing back at her and paying attention to where the boat was going. Thankfully, Lake Lewisville was huge, so there weren't many boats in their path, and they were going really slowly as she surfed. She liked the feel of cruising behind the boat and messing around with the wake.

"If you want to, you can try to find the sweet spot where there's no tension in the rope and then throw the rope in," Xavier called back.

"What? You're crazy!" The short rope's connection to the boat was the only thing keeping her afloat.

"I promise it works. It's easy." He grinned. "You're a natural!"

Izzy played around with moving closer to the boat and then backing off into the wake. Eventually, she found the spot he described. When she was close enough to the boat she felt like she could step onto the wood platform if she wanted, there was a spot where she didn't need tension in the rope to stay there. She messed around with it a little more and slowly coiled the rope then got brave and tossed it at the back of the boat. The rope landed on the padded part. Izzy could feel herself falling back toward the huge wake.

"Pump the board," Xavier called.

She pushed up and down with her front foot and moved back into the spot. This didn't feel like surfing on the ocean as she was pressing against the wave instead of riding with it, but it was a lot of fun. She kept pumping the board when she needed to, and stayed in the spot for maybe half a minute before, inch by inch, she fell back away from the boat. She couldn't catch the wave again, causing her to gently sink into the water. The board popped up, and within seconds, Xavier had circled back to her, grinning so proudly.

"You did it! Seriously, you rocked it. Do you want to try again or maybe try wakeboarding? It's not much harder."

"I'm feeling pretty good for now," she said. "Why don't you go?"

He reached out, and she lifted the board to him. Then she laid back and let her hair float in the water for a few seconds before swimming to the platform and pulling herself out. Her hair was going to be a frizzy mess in seconds, but who cared. This was a great reprieve from her normal life, and she loved sharing it with Xavier. He was definitely not what she'd planned on from their interactions Thursday night or even this morning. He was slowly becoming his real self with her, and she realized she liked him.

Unzipping the life jacket, she caught him staring at her again and gave a saucy flip of her hair. "Really? You going to drool next?" she asked.

"I just might." He gave her a sexy smolder, and her stomach erupted in butterflies.

Xavier took a step closer, and her eyes skimmed over the way his neoprene shirt clung to his muscular chest and arms. Luckily, he hadn't taken his shirt off or she'd be the one drooling.

He slowly walked toward her, and her breath caught in her throat. She had to say something quick or she'd be kissing him again, and she couldn't be moving this fast. "You're going to teach me how to drive then?"

He stopped and arched an eyebrow. "You're ready to drive?"

She looked pointedly around at the empty boat save the two of them. Her heart was still pounding from him almost kissing her again. She wanted him too much, and this date was confusing and making her lose all her inhibitions. She needed to get a grip and quick. "If I don't learn, you won't get to surf. Who usually drives you?"

"One of my buddies from the team, or I have this awesome family that lives next door with three teenage boys, the Jensens, and they love to come out with me. Their dad travels internationally for work, so he misses out."

"I bet they love coming with you."

"They're great kids."

She liked that he seemed to genuinely care about children. The interaction with the redheaded boy outside the restaurant, and the way he'd treated all the young adults they'd played paintball with this morning, demonstrated that. He was a standup guy.

He lifted the board back into place and walked toward the driver's seat. "Okay. You ready for your driving lesson?"

Izzy set the life jacket on a bench seat and walked to him, tucking her hair behind her ear. The water on her skin was evaporating quickly in the heat. Xavier sat on the driver's seat and gestured her closer. Izzy didn't know where to stand, so she came to his side and watched.

"This is the throttle. Just push it forward to go and back for reverse. There's no brake, so I just go into reverse for a second if I need to stop quickly, or you can just idle slowly."

"I'm going to wreck your boat," she said, tucking her hair back again.

Xavier laughed. "No, you won't." He gestured around. "There's a lot of water out here, and my lesson will teach you all you need to know."

She laughed. "But if, by some small chance, your lesson isn't magnificent?"

"Won't happen." He smiled softly as if he guessed her worries. "You only need to drive if you want to."

"But if I don't drive, you can't surf."

He smirked. "I'd rather wakeboard, but it's fine if I don't today. I get lots of chances."

"Okay." She rubbed her hands together, trying to act confident. "Let me at it."

"C'mere." He beckoned her closer, and Izzy gulped as she realized he wasn't going to move out of her way.

She got brave and scooted closer. Xavier took her waist between his large palms, and she gasped. His look said he knew exactly how it affected her to be so close to him. He pulled her between him and the wheel. She was facing him as he sat in the padded driver's seat, and there wasn't a lot of room. She couldn't handle him looking at her like that anymore so she spun to face the wheel, but then she realized she'd just put her rear in plain view and spun back. Xavier was grinning broadly.

"It's okay. I'm not going to bite."

She swallowed and looked out at the dark blue water and a sailboat skimming past. Xavier reached up and touched her cheek gently. She glanced back at him.

"I'm sorry if I'm making you uncomfortable," he said.

Izzy pressed her lips together then admitted, "I don't have a lot of experience with men."

He reared back, shock crossing his handsome features. "Why not?"

She didn't want to get into this, but for some reason, she trusted that he wouldn't downplay her fears. "My father." A tear crested her eyelashes and rolled down her cheek, and Izzy wanted to die with embarrassment. What was this man doing to her—kissing her before she knew him well and bringing out emotions she'd sealed and buried in an embossed coffin a long time ago?

Xavier suddenly stood, his large frame towering over her. She was eyelevel with his chin and leaned back to look up at him. She wondered if he was going to try to kiss her again. Though she wanted to kiss him, the moment wasn't right at all for her.

Instead, Xavier took her hand and led her over to the padded bench running along the side of the boat. They sat, and he held onto her hand and focused on her face. "My dad overdosed when I was three, and my mama never talks about him, so I understand not having the best example of a good father."

Izzy's breath popped out of her. She clung to his hand and then simply leaned her head against his broad shoulder, staring out at the gently rolling waves lapping against their boat and the other boats zooming by. The sun was bright, and there were only a few puffy clouds, but the boat's shade kept them from being too sticky hot.

She opened her mouth, and the thing she never told anybody quickly spilled out. "My mom got stage four breast cancer when I was seven."

Xavier's hand tightened around hers, and the muscles in his arm and shoulder tensed.

"Then while she was fighting through chemotherapy and radiation for over three years, my father cheated on her with the woman who is now my stepmother." She could still see them in the kitchen, hugging. Then her father had looked into Dolly's eyes like Izzy had only seen on the movies and bent his head to kiss her. Izzy had run and hid in her bedroom. Her mom died not long after and her dad completely withdrew from her, not that she minded.

"Oh, Izzy." Xavier released her hand and wrapped his arm around her. She buried her head in the soft fabric of his neoprene shirt, finding safety in the muscles there. She felt like this man could protect her from hurt in so many forms if she could allow him to. "You've gone through so much, and yet, you're this incredible, talented, and hard-working woman."

"Thank you for seeing me like that. Sometimes, I feel like a little girl who still wants her daddy back." She could not believe she'd just admitted that to him. Even her sister and stepmom didn't know how she longed for her daddy. Dolly and Hailey were both so friendly and warm, but after a lot of failed attempts, neither of them tried anymore to delve into her issues with her father.

He rubbed his hand along her bare arm. "I think we all feel like that sometimes." He chuckled. "Little boys and girls."

"I'm glad you have your mama. She seems amazing." She looked up at him.

He nodded. "She is. Do you have anyone?"

What a tough question to ask. Did she? Not really that she could talk to, but she did have love, no matter how many times she'd tried to reject it. "My stepmom, Dolly, loves me unconditionally, even when I was the brattiest teenager you'd ever meet and after I cut myself off from them at eighteen. She and my sister, Hailey, would have none of that." She smiled, remembering how Dolly had shown up at her dorm and told her in no uncertain terms that she wasn't losing her.

Xavier looked surprised. "So the woman your dad cheated with? The blonde who's always at the games with him?"

"Yeah. Weird that I can forgive her but not him, right? But if you met her ..." She wished she could explain the happiness Dolly and Hailey brought to her life. "The woman is just pure sunshine and such a blonde bombshell. She works hard to look like Dolly Parton. It cracks me up, but I don't think anyone could help but love her or my sister." Izzy had tried but failed. The issues with her dad were deeper. Not only had she seen him that time with Dolly in their kitchen when her mom was sick but after her mom died he turned away from Izzy and she had to mourn alone. Only when Dolly and Hailey became a permanent part of her life a few years later, and forced her to let them love her, had she known familial love again.

"I've met your sister. She's a trainer for the team."

"Yeah. She's great. Her and my father get along really well, which is so weird to me, but to each their own, right?"

"So you cut yourself off, but your sister embraced your father's team?" he asked.

"Hopefully not literally."

"No, she's really professional, even though I know a lot of the guys wished she wasn't."

"I bet. Don't you think she's the most beautiful woman you've ever seen? With her blonde hair and perfect body and skin and her big blue eyes, but that little cleft in her chin gives her something different —what?" He was staring at her, and it derailed her thought process.

"No, I don't think she's the most beautiful woman I've ever seen. Not even close." He turned her toward him and raised his other hand and trailed it down her cheek. "No one could be as beautiful as you, Izzy." He slowly lowered his head toward hers, and Izzy's breath caught in her throat. He couldn't be sincere with his compliment. He shelled compliments like that out to different women every day. And yet, somehow, it felt authentic. It felt wonderful.

He was so close she could feel his breath on her lips. He smelled amazing—that mix of musk, lime, and salt. Izzy wanted to be strong and not become another one of his numbers, but he was proving almost impossible to resist. Every nerve in her body was on high alert as he trailed his fingers along the bare skin on her back.

She lifted herself closer to him, and then a wall of water smacked them both in the side of the head. Izzy was knocked away from him and blinked to clear her eyes. The right side of her face felt like it had been sandblasted.

She heard a cackling and whirled to see a blue boat speeding away with a young skier looking back at them and laughing. The teenage boy raised a hand in triumph. "I got you, X!"

Xavier shook his head. "Of all the rotten timing." He stood and opened a compartment next to the passenger seat and handed her a blue beach towel.

She pressed the dry towel against her face. If she had any makeup on after her first attempt at surfing it was gone now. Xavier had basically said she was the most beautiful woman to him. It had to be a line he gave all of his women. She did not want to be just another one, but she was like silly putty that he could mold into whatever he wanted.

"Who was that?" she asked.

"My neighbors, the Jensens, I was telling you about. Looks like their dad's home today and taking them skiing. That was the eighteen-year-old, Brody. See if I ever take him skiing again."

Izzy couldn't help but laugh. It was pretty funny that the kid interrupted their kiss by spraying them with gallons of lake water. It had cooled her off in more ways than one. Ready to not discuss anything serious, and promising herself she wouldn't go for another kiss until she knew for certain Xavier wasn't just toying with her, she walked to the driver's seat. "Okay. I'm ready to try driving."

"Good girl. After I show you my tricks on the wakeboard, I'll ski and swamp Brody's entire boat."

———

It was after dark when they made it back to Izzy's condo after driving through Golden Chick and each getting fried chicken with fries. She was a frizzy, dirty mess from lake water, but it had been the best day she could remember. It had taken her half an hour to get confident enough to drive the boat, but then she'd done all right. Xavier had impressed her with flips and three-sixties on the wakeboard. When he skied, she'd gotten brave enough to get close to the bright blue Tige boat, and Xavier had indeed doused the teenage boys and their dad.

They stopped outside her door, and she preempted whatever he was going to say with "That was the best date I've ever been on."

Xavier grinned, and the porch light picked up his dimples. Oh, mercy. "Me too. I wish I could take you out tomorrow."

She put a hand on her hip. "Well, why can't you?" She was partially teasing, but there was also an underlying worry that he was the player the media made him to be and he probably had another date lined up. This could very well be a one and done experience for them.

He laughed. "I'm flying to Monterrey, Mexico in the morning to help my mama in an orphanage there."

She stepped back. "Wow. Good for you." She'd heard how much he helped the children, but here was actual proof.

"It's a lot of fun. I get to be with the kiddos and my mama and do all the projects they need a tall guy for. Important stuff like changing the light bulbs or dusting the ceiling fans."

"Good to be invaluable like that."

"For sure." He took a step closer. "I'll be back Friday night. Could I plan another date for us?"

She edged closer until they were only inches apart. Yes, he wasn't going to write her off. "I'd like that."

Xavier's arms came around her, and his dark eyes were hyper-focused on hers. She had no clue how she'd stay strong. How was she supposed to guarantee he wasn't a player anyway? Maybe she needed to live life and not worry so much, but the worry ate at her insides as he brushed her hair behind her shoulder, his warm fingers doing a number on the sensitive skin on her neck. He leaned even closer, and his phone started buzzing in his pocket.

He startled and shook his head, pulling it out and pushing a button to stop the buzzing. "My mama." He held it up for her to see. The display said, "Best Mama Ever." "I can call her back."

"It's fine. You should get it." This was the break she needed. She bit at the inside of her cheek to try to compose herself and tucked her hair behind her ear.

"Okay." He pushed out a breath and slid his finger across the screen to accept the call, striding a few paces away. Izzy watched him, feeling awkward observing his personal conversation, but very interested in how he interacted with his mama.

———

"Hello, Mama." Xavier had wanted to sample those rosebud lips again, badly, but his entire life his mama had come first. He really appreciated Izzy understanding and encouraging him to take the call. He'd had a lot of dates who'd been peeved that he put his mama first.

"Well, she has gone and messed up everything now!" Mama roared in his ear.

"Who?"

"The nurse, Holly or something Christmassy like that. I don't know. I'm trying to block her from my memory. She wouldn't know the Christmas spirit if it dumped a lump of coal on her head. Ooh, that would serve her right. I'll be praying for that one from Santie this year. You can bet your butt on it."

Xavier smiled, his heart rate almost back to normal from the thrill of the near-kiss with Izzy. Those two kisses this morning weren't near enough, and he kept getting interrupted. He smiled remembering Brody hitting them with the wave of water. Funny kid but his timing stunk. "What happened?"

"She backed out of the trip a few minutes ago. Last minute, like a little selfish coward! I need someone who can administer the immunizations and give the little ones a checkup. You know how the medical care is down there. Half the time, we show up and one of my sweeties will have a broken arm nobody has set."

Xavier made a noise of assent. Mama never needed much to keep talking, especially when she was upset like this. He glanced over at Izzy. Her dark hair frizzed around her beautiful face. He doubted she had any makeup left after boating, and he thought she was more beautiful than ever as she smiled tentatively back at him. Was she pulling away? At moments, he felt like she was into him. Then her eyes would cloud, or she wouldn't rise to the bait when he flirted with her. He wanted her like he'd never wanted any woman, and he had to convince her he wasn't anything like her father.

"Little brat," Mama continued, "thinks she's got a life that's more important than helping the children she committed to help six months ago. I'll show her a life. And then—you won't believe this baloney—she had the nerve to say to me, 'If you can guarantee that your big handsome stud of a son will come on the trip, I can move some things around and make it work.' Little conniving monster. How dare she? That's why I never tell anybody you're coming. If you ever date a selfish witch like that, I'll make *you* work!"

"Calm down, Mama. Just calm down." It was the line he always gave her when she got like this. When they were together, he would open his arms, and she'd immediately stop ranting.

She grunted out a laugh. "I wish you were here to hug me as you said that."

"Me too, Mama." He glanced up at Izzy, wishing he could hug her, but his Mama obviously needed him. "What can I do to help?"

"You coming will be help enough, sweet boy. I'll figure it out." She barked out an annoyed laugh. "Unless your girl of the day happens to be a qualified RN instead of a supermodel."

"How about an over-qualified one?" He glanced at Izzy, who looked quizzically back at him. His heart started beating hard and fast. Would she do it? He wanted to get to know her better and spend more time with her. Flying to Mexico and spending a week with the children would show exactly who anybody was on the inside, and it might give him the chance to convince her he wasn't a player.

"Even better," Mama said. "Who are you thinking of?"

"Can I call you right back?"

"Of course, love. Oh, I could just hug you!" She hung up before he could respond.

Xavier dropped his phone back into his pocket and turned to Izzy. Could he really ask this of her? She could say no. She probably would say no. But, oh, how he hoped she wouldn't.

"Everything okay?" she asked.

"My mama." He chuckled and brushed a hand over his hair. "She gets a little intense sometimes."

"What happened?"

"We always take a nurse with us on these trips. They're able to update the children's immunizations, do wellness checks, and deal with any injuries that haven't been taken care of, stuff like that."

Her mouth formed an o.

"The nurse backed out last minute." He tapped his thumb against his leg when she still said nothing. "Would you come?" The words rushed out, too quickly, too unconvincing.

Izzy swallowed and stepped back. "Um, well, I would love to help the children, but ..."

He nodded hurriedly. "No, I understand. It's awful to ask you something like this last minute. Don't feel bad that you can't come. You have a job, a life. I'm sorry to put you—"

Izzy stepped forward and clapped her hand over his mouth. "X! It's not an awful thing to ask. It's a compliment that you'd want me." She removed her hand.

Xavier stared at her. Did he dare hope?

"I do want you, Izzy," he said in a husky voice.

Her face flushed. She blinked at him. "How can I be sure you don't just want me for today?"

It was exactly what he thought she'd been concerned about, and he was so glad she'd asked.

Xavier knew words weren't going to work. She'd probably been lied to by her father and other men. He had to show her with more than words, and though he'd loved kissing her this morning, he'd probably damaged her trust instead of gaining it.

"Spending a week with me will show you that I'm not what the media has made me out to be. I'm interested in you, Izzy, not any other woman and I promise I won't push you physically."

Izzy regarded him for almost half a minute. He wanted to talk her into coming to Mexico, but he patiently waited. The military life had taught him patience and then some.

Finally, she looked him up and down. Then a small smile appeared on her rosebud lips. "You know, X, I haven't taken a day of vacation in the two years I've been working at the hospital. I might have to do some finagling with my schedule, but I think I can make it work."

Xavier blinked at her. Then he whooped and picked her off her feet and lifted her high into the air.

Izzy threw back her head and laughed as she was suspended above his head. "I feel like Baby from *Dirty Dancing*."

"I don't know who Baby is, but I could do some—" He cleared his throat, but his voice was still husky. "Dancing with you."

Izzy just laughed harder.

Xavier slowly lowered her until she was pressed against his chest. "Thank you," he whispered. His heart thudded out of control. With any other woman he was interested in, he would've went for a kiss, but Izzy was different. For the first time, he was dreaming of long term, and he knew he had to gain her trust.

Izzy threw her arms around his neck and clung to him. Xavier simply enjoyed holding her and inhaling her gardenia scent. Hopefully, this week he'd have lots of opportunities to get to know her. Once she knew she could trust him, he hoped he'd be able to fulfill all the desires to hold and kiss her that were churning inside him.

She pulled back and looked up at him. "I still have to arrange my work schedule."

"Thank you for making this work."

"And we need to do some serious education if you don't know what *Dirty Dancing* is."

"I told you I can figure that one out." She was flirting with him, and she was coming with him to Mexico. Happiness surged through him, almost as strong as the desire to kiss her again.

"No, you dork. It's a movie, and it's a mixture of salsa and mamba, not some ... well, you know."

"Oh. That's disappointing." He twisted a lock of her hair around his finger. "Bring it on the plane, and we'll watch it."

"I will."

"Then we'll practice the moves every free minute we get."

She smacked his shoulder, but couldn't hide her smile. "I'd better let you go," she said.

Reluctantly, he released her from his arms. She walked to the door and punched in her code. Xavier hurried over to swing the door wide, wishing he could extend the date, but they'd been together all day, and they might be together all next week. It had to be enough for now.

"Thank you for a fantabulous day," she said.

"It has been amazing," he said. "Great date planning on my part."

"Ha! You wanted to take me to the demolition derby and knock me off my princess pedestal."

"I was wrong about you being a princess." He brushed the hair from her neck and cupped her face in his palm. "You're an angel." He stared at her beautiful face for a moment but then backed away so he wouldn't finagle his way inside her apartment. "Mama's gonna love you."

Izzy lifted a hand in farewell. "I'm gonna love her."

Xavier grinned. He was sure of that. Everyone loved his mama. He turned and jogged to the steps.

"X, wait!" Izzy walked back out of her condo, and he had all kinds of visions of cuddling on her couch and watching this *Dirty Dancing* show right now before trying out some dance moves on her. "What time is our flight?"

"Oh, um." Just like that he was slammed back down to reality. "Whenever we want it to be."

"What?" Her brow wrinkled.

How in the world had she come from the home she had and didn't act like she'd ever been on a chartered flight?

"The plane will pick Mama up in Denver tomorrow morning then come get us. We can leave whenever you want."

"Oh, right. Okay. I'll text you when I have the all clear with work." She waved and walked back into her apartment.

Xavier cheesily placed a hand on his heart. Longest and best date of his life, and he hadn't wanted it to end. He pulled out his phone to call Mama back. This was going to be fun.

11

Izzy's stomach bubbled with excitement as the sleek white jet flew over jagged, green mountains then started its descent. She turned to Mama with an open mouth. "It's so beautiful!"

Mama chuckled. "You'd better come visit me in Denver if you like mountains this much."

Izzy had immediately fallen in love with the tall lady, with her dark hair in cornrows and a huge smile on her face. Xavier had definitely gotten his dimples from her.

"I would love that." She caught Xavier staring at her and blushed. She would love to spend more time with Mama and Xavier, but she didn't want to impose. She still couldn't believe she'd been so impulsive and come on this trip. Xavier definitely pulled out her fun, brave, and flirtatious side. Yet she still felt compelled to be careful about giving her heart away. She loved that he'd understood and was trying to show her that she could trust him. She'd been disappointed when he hadn't kissed her last night but appreciated that he was taking it slow, especially after their impulsive kisses that morning. If only she could forget how good those felt.

"Haven't you seen mountains before?" Xavier asked.

"I went to Kauai a couple of times in high school. Hiking to the waterfalls was my absolute favorite thing."

"You'll have to take her to Horsetail Falls." Mama instructed.

"Sure thing," Xavier agreed.

Izzy noticed that he agreed with anything his mama said. Luckily, his mama seemed to have a heart of gold. Izzy already loved her, but she'd never been the type to be obedient, so it was kind of strange to her.

"Why haven't you traveled much?" Xavier asked in a low tone.

She met his gaze. How did he keep drawing things out about her past? She didn't let people in like this. At the hospital, she'd heard that if a doctor wanted to ask her out, another doctor would explain that she had "ice in her veins." Dr. Murphy calling her an ice queen last week confirmed it.

"We vacationed a lot when I was little, but I don't remember it much. After my mom got sick, we just stayed at home and prayed."

Mama's eyes widened. "Oh, sweet girl."

Izzy bit at her lip and gave Mama a nod. "I'm okay." She focused back on Xavier. "After she died, my dad and I did our best to ignore each other. When he married Dolly, they vacationed nonstop with Hailey and always tried to bring me along. I usually threw such a fit they let me stay home. The Kauai trips were the only exceptions. Hailey and I had a lot of fun there. I left home at eighteen, and vacations are a little hard to come by when you're putting yourself through school and starting a career."

She glanced away from their sympathetic looks and out at the industrialized city.

"It's so modern."

Mama nodded. "One of the most modern cities in Mexico, but sadly, there's a huge discrepancy between the upper and lower classes. That's why our help with the children is so invaluable." She squeezed her hand. "Bless you for coming."

Izzy felt blessed just being here with the two of them. Getting the time off work had been surprisingly easy. Since she'd never asked before, and tried to help out when she could, she was able to get other nurse practitioners to cover her shifts without any persuasion.

Things were a whirlwind of activity as the plane landed and taxied down the short runway. Soon, they, their luggage, and boxes of supplies were transferred to a Chevy Suburban. The driver took them directly to the orphanage, New Life, a two-story building with a metal roof and tan siding. There was an open yard with a playset and grass, but the entire area was surrounded by large fences.

"Please don't go outside the fences," Mama asked her. "Unless Xavier and the driver are with you."

"Okay." Izzy nodded quickly, the excitement from earlier diminishing a bit at her serious tone.

"Even if you're out with Xavier, don't look at another man. They will take that as an invitation, and I don't want my boy having to get in a fight to protect you."

Izzy laughed then realized Mama wasn't teasing. "I'm sorry. You're serious?"

"There is a lot of organized crime in the city, and that's terrifying enough, but the men will definitely see you as either an attraction or an opportunity to make money, so be very careful, love."

Izzy nodded.

The car rolled through the gate, and as soon as the gate was shut behind them, Mama jumped from the car and ran for the playground. "Mis hermanas!"

The children saw her and set up a cry of joy of their own.

Xavier got out and offered her his hand. "Don't worry." He smoothed his finger across her forehead.

"Do I look scared?" She felt scared.

"Mama's just trying to keep you safe. I'll protect you."

She felt reassured by his strong, solid presence and turned her attention to the children who were swarming Mama. This was why they'd come. It wasn't a vacation, so staying within the protective walls should be no big deal. Though she had to admit she'd love to see the waterfall Mama mentioned on the plane.

Xavier took her hand and walked toward the children. He didn't get very far before they were running toward them. Xavier released her hand and caught a five-year old boy, tossing him in the air. Two more were reaching for him, and a third was tugging at his pant leg. The first little boy squealed with joy. "X!"

Izzy noticed two girls shyly approaching her, their dark eyes wide. She bent down. "Hola." It hit her how little Spanish she knew. How was she going to communicate?

"Bella señorita," the taller girl said, touching her hand reverently.

"You're the pretty one," Izzy told her.

The girl beamed, and Izzy thought she must've understood.

They eventually went inside and unloaded their suitcases and supplies. Izzy was busy up until dinner. She started again as soon as dinner was finished, doing checkups on the children who needed immediate help. There was a broken ankle she needed to set, which was awful as it had been broken for a while. She dealt with ear infections, a case of tonsillitis, and almost a dozen children who were manifesting AIDS symptoms. The last cases were so heart-wrenching she had to steel her mind and not think about it.

She was exhausted when she finished up and took a quick shower. Mama had shown her the room the two of them would be staying in earlier that day. Dragging her feet along the hallway, she heard a deep voice singing, "Jesus said love everyone ..."

Xavier? The exhaustion fled as she crept toward the nursery and peeked in the doorway. The light from the street outside filtered in the windows. Xavier had an infant cradled against his bare chest and was pacing the tiled floor of the nursery, singing softly. The infant was only in a diaper and Xavier held her close.

Izzy watched him for a while, peace overcoming her. Was he truly this good and kind? He'd wanted her to learn to trust him this week. Moments like this were a perfect start. She forced herself to not drool over the cut lines of his arms, shoulders, chest, and abdomen. She'd seen him without a shirt on yesterday on the boat and been impressed, but this was much more intimate and appealing.

He finally noticed her and tilted up his chin, giving her a soft smile. "Hey," he whispered.

She crossed the distance to him and peered down at the innocent child. Probably only a few weeks old and much too small to be healthy, the baby's eyelids fluttered quickly, and she sucked at her pacifier like she wasn't content.

"Mama said her mother was taking cocaine and meth. So it's hard for our sweet Isabella to settle down and rest."

Izzy jolted, and her eyes flew to his face. "Her name's Isabella?"

"Yes. Isn't she beautiful?"

"She is." He'd stopped pacing but he kept bouncing slightly.

"Skin to skin contact?" she guessed, heat creeping into her face as she let her eyes dip to the sculpted musculature of his abdomen.

He grinned but sobered quickly. "It helps calm her down, Mama's done all the research."

"I'll bet she has." Mama was a force to be reckoned with but everything she did was to help someone else. Izzy adored her. "You're good with all of the children."

"Lots of practice." He grinned, and those dimples dragged her in like always.

"Do you want me to hold her so you can get some rest?" Izzy offered to distract herself. Those muscular arms of his holding a sweet baby were more attractive than anything she'd ever seen.

"No. You're much more important than me."

She started to protest but he shook his head. "Truly. You've already done so much for the children, and tomorrow you'll start the immunizations and that will be tough. You get your rest. Isabella and I will be just fine."

Izzy stepped closer to him and touched his face with her hand. "You're a good man. Thank you for bringing me here."

The words hung between them, and she wondered if he'd try to push her to be with him physically. Other men she knew definitely would.

Instead, he smiled softly. "Thank you for being here, Izzy. These children need you much more than they need me."

"I don't know about that." She glanced down at the baby who had relaxed and was now sleeping peacefully in his arms. She'd seen a lot of babies withdrawing from drugs, and it was vicious. The baby would most likely sleep fitfully through the night, if at all. Xavier was in for a long haul. He was made of much stronger stuff than just his fine-honed muscles. "Goodnight, X."

He focused in on her and smiled. "Goodnight, Izzy."

She turned to leave, surprised at how hard it was to walk away.

12

The next four days passed far too quickly, and before Xavier knew it, Thursday night had crept up on them. They were flying home tomorrow night, and he hadn't had any time alone with Izzy. He'd hoped to show her he could be trusted, but the focus right now needed to be on these children. He didn't have a clue what Izzy was thinking about him, about his hope that they'd develop a relationship.

Izzy had been amazing, taking great care of all the little ones' medical needs and accomplishing much more than other nurses he'd worked with because she had additional medical knowledge and pediatrics training with her advanced degree. She'd needed to use a translator quite often, but Mama and the orphanage workers had been extremely impressed and grateful Izzy was here.

Mama and the two workers who stayed the night at the facility were upstairs putting the little ones to bed. Xavier had sung baby Isabella to sleep. She seemed to be doing better each day. Holding that baby gave him a peace he rarely felt in his busy life. He realized he hadn't even charged his phone down here. He'd noticed a few missed calls from his agent Sunday morning, but he'd ignored him. The guy made him feel slimy and Xavier was done getting setup on dates and trying to project some image. He could deal with his agent and the contract negotiations when he got back to Dallas. The decision between Texas and Denver didn't feel as heavy or pressing since he'd stepped away from the situation. Though he longed to be closer to Mama and be there for little Marcos, if he kept being as impressed as he was with Izzy, and somehow broke through her trust issues, he'd have a much harder time leaving the Titans.

Music floated up from the main floor, and he headed toward it. Traipsing down the stairs, he could hear a familiar song from home that had a Spanish flair and equal parts Spanish and English words. He strode toward the main area, but stopped before he entered the arched doorway. Izzy was dancing with some of the older girls as they giggled and twirled. The way she moved was beautiful and much too appealing to him. She swayed and twisted with fluid movements, her skirt floating out when she spun and her white tank top showcasing her beautiful shape.

"X." One of the girls pointed to him and giggled.

Izzy whirled and saw him. Her face was flushed with exertion and excitement. She literally shone, and the smiles on the girls' faces reflected exactly how he felt when Izzy was around. She brought joy and a spark wherever she went.

Xavier slowly walked toward her, not letting his eyes stray from her beautiful face. She flipped her hair and arched an eyebrow. "Really? You going to drool now?"

Xavier couldn't help but laugh. He reached her side and wanted with everything in him to take her in his arms. He stepped close and lowered his voice. "Is this like your dirty dancing?"

"No!" She laughed. "You really need to see the movie."

"Why didn't we watch your movie on the plane?"

"I didn't dare with Mama right there."

"Oh? It's one of *those* movies." He pumped his eyebrows and lifted the hair off her shoulder, grazing her smooth skin with his fingertips.

"Not really, well, sort of." Her beautiful skin flushed even darker.

"Maybe we can recreate it?" His voice dropped lower so the girls couldn't overhear.

The pulse in her throat throbbed, and she licked her lips, but her answer was a prim. "Not with the children watching."

Xavier reached down and took her hand, the simple touch shot awareness through him. He wanted to dance with her and much more. He turned and waved to the girls who were watching them like a movie screen. "Buenas noches. Dulces sueños. Mama está esperando."

They all groaned with disappointment, but returned the salutations and filtered from the common area.

"What did you tell them?" Izzy's voice was husky as she met his gaze.

"That I needed to be alone with their beautiful nurse so she could teach me how to dirty dance."

She gasped. "You did *not*."

Xavier lifted their clasped hands to his chest and wrapped his other palm around her hip, bringing her body in tight to his. He smiled. "Your willing student, mi bella señorita."

Izzy started swaying her hips to the music, and he tried to follow her, but feeling her movements was distracting him completely. She pulled away from him, but held onto his hand, swinging out and shimmying her torso before swinging back in. Xavier laughed and pulled her close again.

"Now put both hands at my waist."

He complied happily. She leaned back, and he almost dropped her in surprise, but he held on, and she arched so low her hair swept the ground as she swooped from one side to the other. Xavier's breath was coming in short pants, and it was all he could do to keep her waist in his grasp. She came back up and grinned at him.

"Can we do that again?" he asked.

She threw back her head and laughed. Xavier bent down and kissed the pulse in her neck. Izzy stopped laughing abruptly and stared at him, her chest rising and lowering quickly.

"No," she whispered.

"No?"

She shook her head and said, "Now you pick me up by the waist and lift me up high above your head."

Xavier was good at taking orders. He'd done it his entire life with his mama, coaches, and superiors in the military. He didn't mind doing it with Izzy, not at all. He wrapped his palms around her tiny waist and easily plucked her off the ground and lifted her high above his head. She laughed again and straightened out her body like a beautiful arrow above him.

"Now spin," she said.

Xavier smiled at her, hoping he was fulfilling some fantasy or something. He spun a slow circle then carefully lowered her, bringing her in close to his chest. She blinked up at him, those long lashes fluttering appealingly. He studied her, the light sheen on her warm brown skin, and the way her chest rose and fell tellingly. He knew he was affecting her. Her eyes filled with a pleading look, and he hoped she ached for him like he did for her.

"Do I have to say it?" she asked.

He wanted her to say it so badly. He wanted her to want him. "Your wish is my command, mi señorita."

Her eyes fell to his lips then rose again to his eyes. "Now kiss," she said softly.

Xavier's hands tightened around her back, pulling her up and in. She stood on tiptoes and he bent down, capturing her warm lips with his own, inhaling her intoxicating gardenia scent. She moaned so sweetly he didn't know that he'd ever been more enamored. He deepened the kiss and ...

"Oh! Excuse me."

"Mama," he whispered against Izzy's lips. She smiled, and he felt it. They pulled apart and turned to face his mama. This was their first kiss since the two that he had stolen at paintball before he truly knew Izzy. He wanted it to continue all night. Mama's interruption was horribly timed.

"Well, I was going to offer some of my pineapple upside down cake, but I think you two have had enough sugar for the night." Mama winked broadly.

Xavier wrapped his hand around Izzy's hip and pulled her against his side. "A man can never get enough sugar."

Mama arched an eyebrow. "Come on, now, let's have our treat and get some rest. If you two want to see the waterfall, you're going to have to wake up early tomorrow."

Xavier nodded and followed along, Izzy at his side. He always obeyed Mama, but tonight he really didn't want to. He leaned down and whispered so only Izzy could hear, "Was that like your *Dirty Dancing*?"

She looked up at him and smiled sweetly. "It was pretty close. You did good, X."

He tightened his hold on her. "We need to watch your movie soon then practice over and over again."

"Sounds like a plan."

Xavier couldn't think of anything better than having plans with her, especially if they involved ... dancing.

13

The driver took them up to Horsetail Falls and let them out a short distance from the bridge. It was green and lush along the trail. The hike was too short for Izzy, especially with the fact that she hadn't been able to run, lift, or do yoga all week, but she wouldn't complain because she was holding Xavier's hand. Their dance and kiss last night had broken down a lot of barriers in her heart, and she felt like they were almost a couple. It was a strange and wonderful sensation.

Xavier stood so tall and protective of her as they walked along the trail. It was a little unnerving to be out away from the orphanage after being sequestered in there the past five days. Any time she got itchy to move more and wanted to go for a run, she thought of the warnings Mama had issued. She didn't want to be in danger, and she really didn't want Xavier to have to fight to protect her. No matter how strong Xavier was, if the other man had a knife, gun, or even was simply hopped up on drugs, he could hurt Xavier, possibly even kill him.

Shivering slightly, she clung tighter to his hand. He smiled down at her, and she was so taken with those dimples and the sparkle in his dark eyes. It felt like they were in their own world in Mexico and especially here in this beautiful spot. He wasn't the playboy she had imagined, and she'd relaxed and opened up to him more in the short time she'd known him than any man she'd known.

They approached the bridge, and the mist from the falls cooled the air. Izzy glanced up at the waterfall splitting between huge boulders above her and falling down from the rocks. Then she glanced over the other side of the bridge railing where more water cascaded down to the river, about twenty feet below.

Xavier watched her. "Do you like it?"

"It's so beautiful. This is narrow-minded of me, but when I pictured inland, northern Mexico, I imagined barren wasteland, desert, not gorgeous mountains and waterfalls."

He nodded. "I love these mountains. Almost as much as I love the mountains from home. On Sundays, my mama and I used to always drive to Elizabeth, a little town in the mountains near Denver, and go on a hike and bring a picnic. She would buy me a cinnamon roll from Annie's Bakery afterwards." He smiled softly.

Izzy loved his story, but her body tensed. "Do you miss the mountains?" She leaned against the bridge and looked up at the cascading water, not sure if she wanted his answer. What if he went back to Denver and left her after she'd finally learned to trust? She wanted to laugh at herself, but she couldn't. They weren't in a relationship, but for the first time in her life, she wanted to be.

"Yeah, I do," he said. "That's the only problem with Texas—flat."

"But that's why everything's bigger in Texas, right? You can see for miles and miles."

"Try hiking to the top of Pikes Peak, and you can see miles of the most beautiful mountains in the world."

"In the world? That's exaggerating a little bit." She tried to inflect a teasing tone in her voice but failed miserably.

He glanced down at her. "You okay?"

"Sure." She wasn't going to let on that she was worried he would leave Dallas. Though it was common knowledge that he was a free agent and Denver was courting him right now. He probably wouldn't leave his friends and the Triple Threat, right? Could she persuade her father to offer him lots of money? Like she'd ever ask her father for a favor.

He studied her but didn't probe deeper. He turned and looked at the waterfall, gripping the railing with his hands. His t-shirt slid up on his arm a little bit and revealed the TTF tattoo. There it was. He loved his team so much that he wouldn't dream of leaving them. He'd engraved them into his flesh. He wouldn't want to have to get a new tattoo.

She couldn't resist tracing her fingers along the tattoo. He trembled under her touch and glanced down at her, the distance of a few seconds ago disappearing with the warmth in his eyes.

"I love this tattoo." She smiled. "For Texas Titan Football or Triple Threat Forever?"

He shook his head. "Neither actually."

"What?" She pulled her hand back. Dang. Maybe he wasn't as committed to her father's team and staying in Dallas as she'd assumed.

He looked back over the waterfall below. She waited, but he didn't expound. Finally, she couldn't take it any longer. "Are you going to tell me what it stands for then? Don't Ace and Kade have them also?"

He nodded and kept studying the water instead of talking to her. Izzy's shoulders bunched around her ears, and though she appreciated the beauty around them, she couldn't enjoy it with him being cryptic and her realizing that he wasn't committed to his team like she thought he was. What if he did leave for Denver? She loved being around him, and she'd seen such tenderness and charity in him this week. To think, this big tough military man, and nationally-acclaimed football player, adored children and respected and loved his mama. He was just about perfect to her, and he might not be sticking around.

"I understand if you can't share the story." She attempted to be sensitive. There were stories in her past she wouldn't want to share.

He glanced down at her. "I don't think Ace and Kade would care if I shared, but please don't tell anyone else."

"I'm as closed off to social media as anyone you know."

He smiled at that. Still gripping the railing, he spoke quietly. She had to lean closer to hear him over the roar of the water. "Three years ago, Ace, Kade, Tiny Tim, and I were in the rookies."

"Tiny Tim? I don't remember him." Not that she would, she didn't really follow her father's football team, though she enjoyed going to the games when she could.

A ghost of a smile crossed his face, but it was gone quickly. "He was the best."

Izzy didn't miss the was, and her neck tightened. She wasn't one who thrived on sad stories. She tucked her hair behind her ear and stared at the sparkling water.

"We were inseparable. It was kind of a given because we were all the newbies, but Tiny Tim was just a stud. Massive, six eight and over three hundred pounds, but really a gentle giant and so stinking funny. You know those guys who are kind of quiet, but then they say something, and you just bust up—can't hardly believe they said it? That type of guy." He swallowed and looked down at his hands gripping the railing.

Several long seconds passed, and Izzy wanted to pry but she didn't. She didn't want to hear why Tiny Tim was a *was* instead of an *is*. She wished she hadn't asked about the tattoo.

"We all thought he was great, and he was ripping it up on the field. Highest tackles from a defensive lineman for a rookie. But I guess he was a little like all of us."

"What do you mean?" The words rushed out before she could stop them and not be the prying woman.

"You don't get to our level of play without being a perfectionist and pretty hard on yourself. I mean ..." He shrugged. "A lot of the players put off this over-confident persona, and we are confident. We do realize we're talented, but we're also our own worst critic."

It made Izzy's heart hurt to realize that Xavier wasn't as confident as he seemed and that many of the players obviously weren't either. But it made sense, their performance every week and their lives were splayed for all the world to see. They were quite often dissected, analyzed, and picked on. It was probably a miserable fish bowl to live in.

"The night we played New England, he didn't play well at all, and the coach reamed him. He went out partying to help forget about it. Then he tried to drive home by himself." He slowly pulled in a breath then pushed it out. "He was so plastered he drove the wrong way up a freeway ramp, and a semi took out his Jeep."

Izzy gasped, remembering the story now. The guy's full name was Timothy Fuller. Hailey had been in college, not working for the team yet, but she kept track of and idolized all the players. Izzy remembered comforting her after the tragedy.

He rubbed his palm over the tattoo on his bicep. "Kade came up with the idea to get these. The world would think we were shouting our allegiance to Texas Titans, but for us it means Tiny Tim Fuller." He fell silent.

The splashing of the water on the rocks below was their only accompaniment for a few beats then Izzy managed to say, "I'm sorry. That's horribly sad."

He shrugged. "Life, right?"

A group of teenage boys were approaching the bridge, and Xavier gestured for her to walk ahead of him. "You ready to go? We can take the trail above the falls too."

"Sure." The mood was sober and reflective as they walked to the edge of bridge, exchanging greetings with the teenage boys.

Suddenly, several of the boys surrounded Xavier, and three more boys appeared in front of Izzy. A lean kid, probably about eighteen, grabbed her arm and yanked her against his side. He reeked of body odor, and she tried to pull away. His buddy had a knife at her neck before she could escape. Izzy shrank back from the cool metal, her heart pumping hard and fast.

One of the boys was yelling at Xavier in rapid Spanish. She had no clue what he was saying or demanding. Xavier's face was a mask of frustration as his eyes jockeyed from her to the boy speaking. He held his hands up and nodded, returning a volley of words that Izzy still couldn't understand.

The kid holding her wrapped his arms more securely around her waist and sniffed her hair. "Bella señorita," he murmured.

Izzy didn't know if it was possible to be any more terrified as she gagged at his horrible smell. She'd assumed they would want money but his movements and words had her skin crawling and sweat dripping down her chest. The other boy pressed the knife firmly against her throat, and she didn't even dare swallow.

Even if Xavier met their demands, would they let them go? They could slice her open easily, and even though Xavier was strong and much larger than any of them, it would be six against one. Her mind scrambled for some kind of solution, some way to escape.

Xavier slowly put his hand in his back pocket and drew out his wallet. He took out a wad of cash and handed it to the boy who seemed to be the leader. Izzy prayed with everything in her. *Please help us. Please inspire them to let us go.* She didn't know if thieves and would-be murderers could feel inspiration, but she was grasping at anything.

The boy took the bills and peeled them apart, counting them. Izzy held her breath. *Please let it be enough. Push them to let us go.*

The boy finally nodded to Xavier. Then he gestured to the boys holding her. The knife was pulled away from her neck, and she caught a full breath, though her lungs still felt constricted with terror. The boy with his arms wrapped around her dragged her off the end of the bridge. Izzy cried out and heard Xavier hollering behind her.

She was looking down at the smaller waterfall that descended below her into the river with boulders and greenery breaking the surface of the water.

"Adios," the boy whispered in her ear before shoving her over the edge.

Izzy screamed, her stomach swooping as she slipped over a large boulder and thumped against another boulder before plunging into the fast-moving river. The water closed over her head, and the current sucked her down. She slammed into another boulder, but she couldn't drag herself out of the current and get any air. Her lungs were constricting, and the need to draw a breath became overwhelming. Pressure built in her head. Darkness closed in tighter and tighter. There was nothing she could do but pray.

————

XAVIER'S HEART WAS BEATING OUT OF CONTROL AS THE BOY ACCEPTED the money and nodded to him then gestured to the kids holding Izzy. The stinking punks. As soon as Izzy was safe, he was going to chase them down and pummel each of them individually.

The knife was removed from Izzy's neck, and Xavier felt the tension in his shoulders ease a little bit, but not enough. He wanted her safe and far away from these losers. He walked toward her, assuming the kid would push her in his direction then run to try and get a head start before Xavier came after them. The kid didn't even glance at him as he dragged her off the bridge and shoved her over the edge.

"Izzy!" Xavier screamed as all the boys rushed around him and sprinted away.

Xavier ran to the edge, watching in horror as her body bounced off a boulder then went under the water. His reaction was probably the stupidest one possible as he scrambled over the lip and leapt into the river. Luckily he cleared the boulder she'd hit, but he hit the bottom of the fast-moving river and jarred his legs. Pushing off, he surfaced and searched everywhere for Izzy. Could he get to her in time? Was she still under the water?

He swam down the current, trying to avoid the boulders but slammed against a few. He spotted her dark hair floating in the water and swam as quickly as he could toward her. She was still under. No, oh, no!

Xavier's arms and legs beat at the cool water and within seconds he'd caught her. He grabbed her around the waist and flipped her over. Her eyes were closed, and his every fear was confirmed.

"No!" He screamed out.

Dragging her to the side, he lifted her up onto the bank and pulled himself out of the water. He rolled her onto her back and tried to remember his first aid training. He heard shouts above him. Horsetail Falls was a popular spot. Maybe some tourist with better training than him would come help, but it was doubtful. He put his cheek against her nose and waited impatiently, but there was no soft exhalation. Despair blanketed him, and the bright sun seemed to be hiding behind clouds. He uttered a silent prayer, simply, *Please help.* Then he pushed his fingers against her neck. Her pulse thrummed against his fingertips, and the cloud parted for a few rays of sunshine.

As quickly as relief hit him, his mind scrambled for what to do now. Izzy would know exactly what to do. Why hadn't he begged her to teach him? Why couldn't he remember the best reaction from the few classes he'd taken in the military on emergency situations? She had a pulse, but she wasn't getting oxygen, and her brain could already be damaged from the lack of air. *Oh, somebody help.*

Rescue breathing? That was the answer, right? He remembered somebody had told him that was outdated now and the first responders should always just do chest compressions. But the rescue breathing just felt right. She needed oxygen. He tilted her head back and plugged her nose, taking a deep breath then exhaling fully into her mouth. He repeated it five times and then stopped to evaluate.

His heart was thumping out of control, and his body was encased in sweat. Why didn't someone come? He glanced up and could see two men working their way down the bank to get to them, but it was precarious, so they had to move slowly.

He checked her pulse again, and thankfully, it was still strong. He put his cheek against her nose, and his stomach plummeted. Still nothing! One of the men finally reached them.

"She's not breathing," Xavier said frantically.

The man didn't reply. He knelt behind Izzy and pushed her over to her side. Izzy immediately vomited river water all over the place. Xavier jumped out of the way, but immediately rushed back to be close to her.

Izzy curled into a ball and moaned. She looked miserable and beat up, but she was breathing.

"Gracias," Xavier said to the man then immediately told the Lord, *Thank you.*

He didn't know if he dared touch her or hold her, but that was all he wanted to do.

The man muttered, "De nada" and stepped back to give them some space.

Izzy sucked in a breath and pushed it out, struggling to sit up. Xavier held onto her arms and helped her into a seated position. She stared up at him, her eyes wide and panicked. "The boys. The river." Her voice was raspy.

Xavier couldn't resist any longer. He sat back against a boulder and lifted her onto his lap, cradling her close. "It's okay. I've got you. You're safe."

She leaned against him, and her entire body trembled.

He cupped her face with his palm. "Are you all right? Do I need to do something medically for you?" Maybe holding her wasn't the best course of action right now. He'd made the wrong choice with rescue breathing, and now, he might be hurting her worse.

She blinked as if debating but nodded. "I think I'm okay. I'm going to have some bruises, but nothing's broken."

"Thank heavens," Xavier whispered against her forehead, pulling her in close again. He glanced up at the two men watching them. "Gracias," he said again.

The men nodded to them and faded away. Xavier wished he was in America as someone would have the EMTs on their way who could make sure Izzy was okay. She'd said she was all right though. He was just going to have to trust her self-assessment. Right now, he simply wanted to hold her until his mind caught up and fully registered that she didn't have brain damage or a broken body.

Her shoulders shook harder, and he glanced down. Tears streaked her cheeks, mixing with the wetness from the river. He gently rocked her. "You're okay." He kept repeating, willing it to be true.

After a few minutes, she seemed to calm and glanced up at him with those liquid, dark eyes. "How did you get to me?"

"I jumped in." He looked back at the waterfall above them with the twenty-foot drop from the bridge and realized it had been a stupid move, but at the time, there hadn't been a choice. He'd do anything to protect her.

Izzy took a long breath and wiped the moisture from her face. "I always knew Xavier was a superhero, but that's pushing it a little bit."

Xavier grunted out a surprised laugh. "I just reacted."

"Thank you." Her eyes sought the ground. Then she muttered, "I was so certain I was going to die. You know those stories you hear about people who are dying?"

He nodded. How close had she come to dying? He shuddered, imagining her thrashing in the water, trying to get to the surface. She must have inhaled water as she fought to breathe and tried to break the surface of the water. *Stop,* he commanded his brain.

"Everything was growing darker. I wanted to suck in air so badly. Then I saw my mom walking toward me. She was so beautiful. I wanted to be with her." She sighed and stopped.

Xavier simply held her. He couldn't imagine how much she missed her mother and what it would be like to see her. He'd often wished he could see his dad, but he probably would've slugged him in the gut, not thought how beautiful he was.

"I did want to be with her," she said. "But I didn't want to die."

"I'm glad to hear that." He kissed her warm forehead, resting his lips there. His body shuddered. "Thank you, Lord, for protecting Izzy," he murmured.

Izzy glanced up at him. "I should've known you'd be a prayer." She traced her hand over his cheek. "I like everything I learn about you X."

He smiled. "I feel the same."

Resting her head against his chest, she cuddled into him. Xavier held her until his body started to feel stiff, and he realized Mama would probably be worrying about them. "We'd better get back to the orphanage and let Mama fuss over you. Do you think you can stand?"

"I'm okay, X." She smiled up at him so sweetly he wanted to protect her from every wrong for the rest of their lives. Whew. He was getting a little sappy, but they'd gone through something horrific, she finally seemed to trust him, and he cared for her far too much.

Xavier gently lifted her to her feet, standing up next to her. Izzy gingerly stepped over the uneven ground. Xavier wrapped his arm around her waist and assisted her. Relief was so strong he wanted to drop to his knees and praise the Lord. Izzy was all right. Nothing else seemed to matter but that.

14

Mama made a huge fuss over Izzy when they made it back to the orphanage. She forced her to drink chamomile tea, take a bath, and take a nap. But Izzy couldn't sleep. She lay on the bed watching the fan rotate and hearing the children's laughter outside her window. Her mind switched between her mother's face and Xavier's. She had wanted her mother so badly, but what she hadn't told Xavier was she had chosen to walk away from her mother and toward him. She'd felt his presence, his arms, even though she wasn't really conscious. When she'd opened her eyes to his handsome face, she knew she'd made the right choice, even though it ripped her apart to not have chosen her mom.

She wanted to tell Xavier exactly what had happened and the choice she'd made, but it seemed too personal, too much too soon. They'd only known each other a week. Was it truly only eight days ago that she'd purchased him at that auction and he'd been irresistible, exhilarating, and terrifying to her? Now, she didn't know where they stood, or if he would even be around next year. Not that she was opposed to a long-distance relationship, but they didn't even have a relationship yet. At least, they hadn't talked about where they stood, and she didn't want to push him. She hadn't even been certain she could trust him, but after this week, how could she not? There was too much to think about, and her mind whirred faster than the ceiling fan.

The afternoon dragged by, but the time did pass. Before she knew it, she'd packed up her suitcase and said goodbye to the children. Then they were on the plane headed home.

As soon as the plane gained altitude and leveled off, Xavier turned to her. "Are you feeling okay?"

"Yes, thank you."

"Can I get you anything?" Mama asked.

Izzy smiled. "I'm really fine." If only she could get Xavier alone and talk to him. Tell him that she trusted him and wanted him to stay in Texas. It would be brave of her, but she could do it.

Xavier studied her with that smoldering stare that made her stomach tumble with anticipation. She shivered and wished, again, that they were alone. Not that she didn't love Mama being around, but she had interrupted their kiss last night and Izzy needed much, much more of Xavier's lips on hers.

"Are you cold?" he asked.

Izzy laughed. "You two, stop worrying. I'm fine."

"You almost died this morning, love." Mama reminded her.

The shiver turned to a tremble.

"Mama," Xavier said quietly.

"Sorry." Mama shook her head. "I'm still trying to process it all."

Izzy squeezed Mama's hand. "It was scary, but X was there for me." She smiled at him.

He grinned in return, and those dimples were beckoning to her. The moment would've been amazing, but it became a little awkward with Mama smiling back and forth between the two of them as if she'd arranged the entire relationship.

"Don't mind me," she said. "I think I'll just take a little nap." She leaned back and closed her eyes.

"Do you believe she's going to sleep?" Xavier asked.

"Not for a minute," Izzy said.

Mama grinned but kept her eyes closed.

Xavier studied Izzy, and she flushed with warmth. His eyes strayed to his mama, and he gave a small laugh. "I think I'll check my emails and texts while Mama takes her nap." He winked at Izzy.

Mama's smile widened.

Izzy tucked her hair behind her ear. If Mama truly fell asleep, she might get the alone time with Xavier she was craving. Oh, to admit that she wanted a relationship with him and then to kiss those full lips and explore those dimples and the muscles in his chest and shoulders. My, oh my, it was warm in this airplane.

Xavier gave her another smile then turned to the phone that he'd plugged into an outlet. She hadn't seen him with his phone all week, and she hadn't bothered with hers. It had been a nice break from reality, but now, they were headed back to the real world. Could their budding relationship withstand the media, her father, and whatever else was awaiting them?

Mama's face relaxed, and her breathing evened out. She was truly asleep. Izzy studied Xavier's handsome face, willing him to glance up and maybe gesture with his chin to the rear of the plane. They could sit side-by-side, hold hands, talk about the children from the orphanage and their adventures, especially the scare this morning. Maybe she'd get daring enough to talk about the trust she felt for him, or maybe they could watch part of *Dirty Dancing* and plan when they could practice the moves. She felt warm all over remembering dancing with him last night.

Xavier's jaw tightened as he read something on his phone. His eyes jerked up to hers, but they were full of concern instead of desire. His phone buzzed, and he checked the screen then glanced up at her again. "Excuse me, I need to take this."

"Of course, no worries." She watched him stand and walk toward the rear of the plane, speaking in hushed tones she couldn't overhear. He kept glancing up at her from time to time.

Something was going on, and from the sinking feeling in the pit of her gut, it wasn't a good something.

He finally ended the call, but he didn't come back for her. Izzy waited several long minutes until she couldn't take it any longer. She stood. His eyes snapped to hers. He shoved a hand over his short hair and gave her a weak smile. She walked to him and stopped right in front of him.

"Everything okay?" Her voice was too quiet, and she felt scared and small. They'd had a powerful week together, why wasn't it enough? Why did it feel like he was pulling away before they had the chance to really come together?

"No, not really." He pushed out a breath. "My agent is a control freak and a complete worry wart. Truthfully I don't like the guy at all, but maybe he's right this time."

"Right?" Izzy squeaked out. "Right about what?"

"Mr. Newton,"—the flight attendant interrupted them—"we're beginning our descent into Dallas. Can you please take your seats?"

Xavier nodded shortly and gestured for her to go first. Izzy's heart was beating almost as hard as when the boy had grabbed her by the waterfall, and she didn't even understand why. What was his agent telling him? What was going on? There were bound to be pictures circulating of her and Xavier from Ace's family's restaurant and their date last Saturday, but she wasn't sure why his agent would care or what he could be right about. Xavier had a different woman on his arm every other day. That was something she hoped was about to change, but she needed to find a way to shrink this distance between them first.

They both took their seats and buckled up.

"What's going on?" Izzy asked.

"My agent is very concerned—"

"Oh, good morning, my loves." Mama stretched and smiled sleepily. "Are we there already?"

"Yep, it's a quick flight." Xavier smiled at his mama, but Izzy could see the tension in his eyes.

Mama looked back and forth between the two of them, seeming jolted by the change in atmosphere from when she'd fallen asleep. "Everything okay?"

"Oh, yeah, of course."

The plane decelerated sharply. Izzy caught a breath from the lack of altitude, or Xavier's outright lie to his mama, she wasn't sure which.

Mama focused on Izzy. "Are you coming back to the house with us? Xavier always has his kitchen stocked. I'll make you some delicious hometown food. I'm craving chicken, shrimp, and veggies after eating beans and rice all week."

"Um, Mama, I have to go meet with my agent and Mr. Knight when we land."

Izzy's stomach swooped. Whatever had upset Xavier involved her father. No! Wasn't it enough her father had betrayed her mom and deserted Izzy when she needed him most? Did he have to ruin the first real relationship she'd had too? She was jumping to conclusions. Xavier had to meet over contract negotiations. It surely had nothing to do with the two of them, and there she went thinking she and Xavier were a couple when that wasn't really true.

"Oh, okay. Izzy and I will get dinner started and hang out." Mama patted her hand.

Izzy stared at Xavier, willing him to reveal something, give her a bit of encouragement about them, anything.

He gave her a look that was filled with longing but then he said, "Can we can take a rain check for tomorrow night? I don't know how late I'll be."

Izzy didn't know what the proper response would be. Xavier didn't want to be with her.

Mama's mouth opened, but it closed quickly. She held onto Izzy's hand as if she sensed Izzy was going to get ripped out of their lives. "Okay, that will be real fine. We'll plan on that."

The plane bumped slightly as it landed and the pilot braked. The plane stopped, and the attendants gathered their luggage and transferred it to the waiting car. Thank heavens it was a private airport, so there was little risk of paparazzi. Izzy wanted so many questions answered, but how did she push Xavier to engage in a deep conversation with her when he'd suddenly become so distant? This cavern between them hurt worse than the bruises from being pushed off the bridge this morning.

She wished she knew what he thought his agent was right about and why he was meeting with her father. The dread in her stomach wouldn't let up. Especially when they got to her apartment and Xavier and his mama both walked her to the door. They each gave her a hug and a lot of thank yous, but nothing more. It definitely felt like goodbye, and she didn't even know what she'd done wrong. As she walked inside, the musk and lime of his cologne seemed to linger. Longing for Xavier filled her, and she wondered if she'd finally given her trust away ... to the wrong man.

15

X avier's gut churned as he walked back to the car with his mama. Izzy had seemed so confused when he'd asked if they could take a rain check, and he wished he could reassure her that everything was fine, but everything wasn't fine. He hated coming back to reality, and reality had slugged him hard when he got on the plane and checked his phone for the first time in almost a week. It was going to be fine, he kept telling himself. He'd get it all figured out with his agent and Mr. Knight. Then he'd go find Izzy and apologize for not being with her tonight. Tomorrow they'd spend the entire day together. Tomorrow everything would be better.

He and Mama got in the back seat of the car. After he gave the driver his address, he turned, ready for the cuss-out.

"What in the crimony is going on with you, boy? That is the best woman you have ever had on your arm, and you are screwing everything up."

Obviously, he didn't have to wait long. The driver tensed as if he didn't want to hear this conversation. This was a professional company Xavier had used before when he didn't want to leave one of his vehicles at the airport. The man knew he'd get in big trouble if he spread gossip about clients, but Xavier still didn't want somebody listening in.

He held up a hand and tilted his head toward the front seat. "Mama, this isn't the time."

She scowled and sat back, folding her arms with a loud harrumph. "You'd better figure out what it's time for, son, before you lose that girl and every chance of happiness you've ever had." She turned away from him and glared out the window, muttering, "I fake falling asleep and he messes everything up."

Xavier couldn't remember the last time his mama had been upset with him. He'd learned very young that obedience brought lots of blessings where his mama was concerned, and he'd always toed the line. Sure, as a teenager he'd gotten into some situations that had upset or scared her and she'd yelled at him, but usually, he was a good obedient boy, and she doted on him and bragged about him enough to annoy anybody who listened for very long.

His mind swung back to Izzy. He wasn't trying to mess things up, but his agent had some valid points and was ticked at him for leaving the country and turning his phone off. They were in the middle of contract negotiations between the Texas Titans and Denver Storm, and here he had pictures all over social media of him on a million-dollar, all-day date with the owner of the Titan's daughter. It had also obviously leaked to the media that he and Izzy were in Mexico together. Of course, they didn't focus on the humanitarian mission and all the good they accomplished. Everything his agent said sounded like the world thought he and Izzy had gone away for a week as lovers. The owner of the Denver Storm was livid, and Xavier's agent didn't blame him. Would Denver's owner pull his offer? If he did, everything Xavier and his agent had worked for would go up in smoke when James Knight realized he had sole control over him and felt no need to up his offer to keep Xavier in Texas. What if there was any truth to his agent's rants that Izzy had bought him at that auction and continued dating him to help her father manipulate him? Out of everything his agent had said, that thought dug at him the worst.

They arrived at his house, and Xavier walked his mama up to the front door and let her in. The driver brought up their suitcases, and Xavier gave him a generous tip, hoping he caught the message to keep his mouth shut.

Closing the nine-foot door behind him, he exhaled, ready for it, but Mama simply glared at him.

He flicked his thumb against his pants. "I've got to go meet with my agent and the owner of the Titans, Izzy's father, and see if we can work out this contract, or if I'm going to accept Denver's offer."

His mama studied him. "It's not Izzy's fault who her father is."

"I realize that, but it sure makes a mess when my agent is ticked at me, and the owner of Denver wonders why I'm dating the other owner's daughter when we're trying to negotiate a contract." He shoved a hand through his hair. "I'll just have to talk to Izzy about waiting to date more until this is settled."

"You know I'd love to have you in Denver and heavens knows Marcos respects and obeys you better than he does me."

Xavier's head shot up. "Is he struggling more?" Their young neighbor in Denver was a prime target for drug runners and gangs. He seemed to listen when Xavier told him to stay far away from those traps, but Xavier wasn't with him near enough.

"He is." She shook her head, and suddenly, she was far away. "But there are children here you can help too."

Xavier was tugged by Marcos. The children he helped here lived in a million-dollar home, and though their father was gone a lot, they were good kids and were going to do great things. Marcos' father had never been part of his life, and while his mama tried she was gone too much. Marcos would be in huge trouble if someone didn't rescue him.

Mama touched his arm. "Maybe you could save Marcos, but maybe you couldn't, and you know I'm watching out for him. You've got to do what's right for you and for your heart."

He shrugged and looked down at his hands, not sure where his heart was or if that really could figure into the equation when you were dealing with your career and the opportunity to have more money than anyone had a right to have. He didn't need the money, but he had a lot of plans to invest and then share the money with those children in need, and Marcos was as important to him as any child.

Mama puffed up, grabbed his shirt, and pulled him down toward her. "That girl is an angel, and if you mess things up with her over some asinine contract negotiation, I will kick your rear end to kingdom come. You got that?" She released him and huffed like a mama bear.

Xavier straightened and didn't know how to respond. His mama was always on his side, not someone else's. He had no desire to mess things up with Izzy, and Mama was correct that none of this was Izzy's fault, but at the same time, was it? Why had she bought him at that auction? Her father had given her the money. She claimed it was all for her hospital and that she hated her father, but he was just taking her word in all of that. All he knew was he needed to figure out the contract. Then he could figure out things with Izzy.

His mama tapped the tattoo on his right arm. "You've got a brotherhood borne out of loss, pain, and a whole heap of hard work. Think about them as well when you're talking dollars and cents, you hear?"

"You don't want me in Denver?" He did love his brothers, but he loved his mama more.

Mama grabbed his arms and tried to shake him, but wasn't strong enough. "I want you happy!"

"Then why won't you move here?" Things would be perfect if Mama was here.

"My place is in Denver, sweet boy. If Marcos and some of those other children didn't have me, they really would go to heck in a hand basket." She tapped his cheek. "But your place is wherever you can be happy. Maybe someday I'll move in next door and watch your babies while you take your wife out to dinner, but right now, I'm needed in Denver, and for once in your life, you need to not worry about obeying a coach, an owner, an agent, a higher-ranking officer, or even your mama. You need to decide if this is your spot and where you can make the most difference and be the happiest. Do you understand me?"

Xavier blinked, and a bit of moisture rolled down his cheek. His mama could do that to him sometimes. He bent down and wrapped his arms around her, whispering in her ear, "Just calm down, Mama. Just calm down."

She laughed and squeezed him tight. Then she released him and gave him a push toward the back of the house. "Go shower, say a prayer, and go to that meeting. You decide what is best for you, love."

"I'll try, Mama."

She shook her head. "I'll be here cooking. You think Ace and Kade will come eat?"

"We might be able to convince them." But if he got through this meeting and figured things out, the person he'd want to be with was Izzy. That thought slowed his steps as he jogged toward his bedroom to shower and carried through as he got dressed, said his prayer, and drove toward the stadium. He'd dated hundreds of women, but he'd never wanted to put one of them before his mama.

The owner's office looked out over the stadium and the Trinity River beyond the green space south of the city. You could look the other direction and see straight to downtown from here too. His agent had been waiting at the elevator and had given him an earful about being influenced by Knight's daughter, how they were probably going to get low-balled now because Knight would think he had Xavier whipped, and how all his hard work of playing Denver and Texas against each other was a waste if he was in Knight's daughter's back pocket. Xavier had listened without comment. It was his agent's job to rant and worry. It was his job to play football, and he'd done his job well this past year. He just wished he knew where he should choose. Izzy pulled at his heart, but so did Marcos and his mama and all the other children she helped on a daily basis.

The door swung open, and Mr. Knight himself waited. "Xavier, come in, son. Come in." He greeted him with a wide smile on his craggy face, extending his hand. Xavier shook his hand but found himself wanting to punch the guy. Son? This was the man who had betrayed Izzy's mother, and she hated him. How dare he act like he and Xavier were tight now?

Knight extended his hand to Xavier's agent, Neil. "James Knight, nice to meet you in person."

Neil had been raving against the man ten seconds ago, but now, he shook his hand with a happy grin. It was hard to resist Knight's magnetism. The guy was powerful and rich, but he was also charismatic, even if his face did look like it'd been carved by a five-year old with a sense of humor.

"You too, sir."

Knight gestured them into his office. His lawyer was in the corner, and he stood and crossed the room, shaking each of their hands. "Garrett Klein." He got right down to business. "Mr. Knight has a formal dinner with his wife and daughter tonight, and we don't want to make him late. Shall we look over the contract and get it signed?"

Everything about that sentence bugged Xavier. As if Knight only had one daughter? And who had said Xavier was going to be happy with the contract and sign it tonight, without even meeting with Denver and seeing their official offer?

"My understanding was we would look over the contract and see if we needed to make any adjustments," Neil interjected.

"I'm really in no rush." Knight spread his arms benevolently. "Whatever we've got to do to keep the best wide receiver in the nation on our team, we'll do." He gave Xavier a smile like a doting uncle.

Whatever they needed to do? Did that include manipulating him into dating Izzy? Was his agent right and Izzy and her father were playing him? Xavier's neck muscles tightened. Izzy wouldn't be part of something like that, would she? He pictured her giving a little girl a hug after she'd administered an immunization shot. Tears had been streaking down the girl's face from the needle, and when Izzy had glanced at him, her eyes had been bright and full of sympathy. No, the Izzy he knew could never be part of a trick to keep him in Texas.

"What if the contract in Denver is more appealing?" Xavier shouldn't have said it, but the challenge was out there before his agent could stop him.

The room went silent, and everyone's smiles froze.

Knight recovered first. "Come now, you know Denver's got nothing as appealing as us."

Xavier's jaw clenched, and he couldn't stop himself from saying, "You mean Izzy?"

Knight blinked at him and then repeated her name softly. "Izzy?"

"Did you set it all up?" Xavier balled up his fist. "Her buying me at that auction? Her being so perfect for me."

Knight actually gave him a genuine smile. Then his face returned to its craggy lines again, and he splayed his hands. "I was talking about my boys, the Triple Threat, our dedicated coaches and fans, and this beautiful stadium." He gestured out the picture window. "We want you here, X, and we'll do anything we need to do to keep you here."

Xavier simply stared at him. Anything. Knight would do *anything* to not break up the Triple Threat and to keep bringing in millions upon millions of dollars and win after win. Nobody could touch their team right now, and Xavier loved that, but he didn't love the feelings he was getting from Knight, and the guy calling him X royally ticked him off.

"Why don't we look over the numbers," the lawyer said, gesturing toward the table where drinks and snacks sat next to a large stack of papers.

"I don't think I'm ready for that yet." Xavier backed away.

Knight's face blanched like somebody had shredded his trump card. "You don't even want to know the offer?"

Xavier faced him head on and said exactly what had been begging to come out for the last five minutes. "I'm ninety-nine percent sure that Izzy is an angel and you are the devil. I don't know what your play is, but you aren't pushing me around, and I will look at the papers when I'm convinced that you didn't offer up your daughter to try to keep me on your football field."

He turned on his heel and strode from the office.

"I love my daughter and would never take advantage of her like that." Knight's voice rang behind him loud and clear.

Xavier spun and marched back in, ignoring his agent and the

lawyer who were both looking completely unsure of their roles at the moment. "My mama taught me respect for my elders, and you'd better be grateful for that right about now. Don't you ever claim to love your daughter. You've ripped her apart, and until I figure out exactly where Izzy and I stand and if she had any part in your scheming, I won't play one more game for you."

He whirled around again and didn't stop this time, even when he heard raised voices behind him. He was in his Bugatti Veyron, speeding away from the field when his phone rang. His agent. He was surprised it took him that long. He debated not getting it, but he had ignored the guy for the past week, and the man had worked for the past four years to get to the point where they would get the offer that was probably sitting back on that table. Had Xavier really walked away from it? And was it because he was mad or because he was defending Izzy?

He pushed the button on his steering wheel. "Neil."

"I can't believe you just did that."

"Hey. I'm screwing up all over the place this week apparently. Dating the owner's daughter, telling the owner off. Shall we just accept Denver's offer and be done with it?" He was being sarcastic, but saying the words felt like a punch in the gut. He didn't want to leave Izzy. He didn't want to leave Kade, Ace, or any of his teammates. He loved the coaches and the Titan fans. He loved his house and neighborhood. He loved his crazy buddies next door.

"Do you even want to hear the offer?" Neil sounded as giddy as a teenage girl asking her friend if she wanted to hear the fanfare her boyfriend had orchestrated to ask her to Prom.

Did he? Yeah. He hated himself for it, but he wanted to hear what Knight thought it was worth to keep him here.

"Sixty-two million for the next four years!" Neil was giddy, and he had a right to be. He'd get his three percent. But that wasn't much compared to the money Xavier would get. He pulled off the freeway and into a gas station, leaning his head back against the cushioned seat.

"Say something." Neil demanded.

"What do you think Denver will offer?"

"I'm going to leak this news to the right people." Neil cackled happily. "If we can prove that you're not already wrapped around Knight's daughter's finger, Denver will match or beat this. I'm sure of it. We can push them over sixty-five easily."

Xavier exhaled slowly. The money was unreal, but what about Izzy? What about Marcos? Where should he go to help those who truly needed him? The offer had his hands shaking. "Why does Knight want me so badly?"

"Hey. I've made you into the most desirable player out there. Oh, and speaking of that, I've got a date for you with Alexandria Fortunata tonight. Drinks at Taylor's Lounge."

"No. Nuh-uh. I'm done with that crap. The offer is there. It's more than either of us planned on. Almost as high as anyone else in my position. I'm done dating every girl to make up some image for you." That was if he planned on staying in Dallas. He kept picturing Marcos' dark eyes sparkling at him when he caught the football Xavier had tossed to him. What if those eyes went dull from drugs? He was only eight.

"Denver's offer hasn't come in yet, and they were ticked about you dating Knight's daughter. One picture of you with Alexandria splayed around the internet and Denver will relax and Knight will realize you aren't in his back pocket. He thought he was playing you having his daughter leech on you, but you played him tonight my friend, and you're going to keep on playing him. We have a week to decide, and when word of this leaks and Denver sees you aren't stuck with Knight's daughter, they can decide if they want to step up to the plate for the most desirable wide receiver in the NFL."

Xavier didn't answer. It all sounded good. It was what he'd worked for the past four years and that was after coming off of two years of active service. Not playing or practicing had been tough and a lot of teams had seemingly forgotten about him and were focused on the players fresh out of college. But he'd fought to be the top in the game, to be so desirable he was offered the highest wage, an absolutely insane amount of money, and to have the choice of where he played.

It needed to be the choice that was best for him and his opportunity to help the children, but Izzy was like an exotic island he dreamed of never having to leave.

"I can't do that to Izzy."

"Izzy!" Neil scoffed. "This has nothing to do with Isabella Knight."

"I just can't. She has trust issues." Xavier shook his head. He was still worried if Izzy had been part of this deal with her father but no matter what he couldn't hurt her. He cared for her far too much.

"You are going to meet Alexandria there in fifteen minutes or I'll shout to the world how Izzy paid a million dollars to sleep with you and you walked away because you wanted to give Denver and Texas each a chance with contract negotiations. You'll look like the saint and she'll be ridiculed, especially when I reveal the proof that you moved on really quickly." He barked a laugh. "I'll doctor up some old pictures of you and Malia dancing that will make your little Izzy bawl. Nobody will be able to see Malia's face, but they'll be convinced that she has no clothes on."

"You wouldn't. Nobody would believe you." Xavier wanted to hurl. He'd put nothing past Neil.

"I'm your stinking agent, everybody will believe me. I've got the pics and I'm really good with Photoshop."

Would Izzy believe him or some slimy pictures? "Why, Neil?" Xavier cleared his throat. He couldn't let this happen. "Why do this for a few million more?"

"I'm gonna get you an offer of sixty-eight million. More than anybody in your position. I'll take my three percent and we'll part ways and players will be lining up to sign with me." He chuckled. "And you'll never dare say anything."

Xavier swallowed hard.

"Man up, X. A couple of innocent pictures with Alexandria or the sleazy shots with Malia and me making Izzy look like she tried to buy your love?"

Xavier's stomach was pitching and he couldn't stand the thought of Izzy's face if she saw the doctored pictures he knew Neil was capable of, not to mention Neil making her look like she'd tried to buy him for completely different purposes than she had. Well, Xavier still hoped it was all for the hospital not for her father's football team.

"And you'll say nothing to anybody. I think Izzy will forgive you going for drinks with a friend, not so sure she'll want anything to do with you after she's been lambasted by the press and the pics with Malia come out. I know she doesn't enjoy the limelight."

Xavier clenched the gear shift in his hand, wishing it was Neil's head. Why had he ever signed with this slime ball? But he had to protect Izzy. He wished he could say no one would believe Neil, but all of this coming from his agent would be pretty strong evidence against him and Izzy.

"Stop," Xavier commanded in a low growl. "I'll do the pics with Alexandria, but as soon as we sign a contract I want you out of my life."

"Sure thing, as long as you promise not to breathe a word of this to Izzy. She's in her father's back pocket and they could ruin everything for us with Denver."

"Whatever," Xavier grunted.

"You shouldn't be too far away from Taylor's Lounge, and you only have to stay long enough to get a few pictures. Happy dance, baby." Neil hung up.

Xavier sighed and dug at the ache between his eyes. He wanted to get home and eat Mama's food and go to bed. He really wanted to go pick up Izzy, go eat Mama's food, cuddle, and watch Izzy's *Dirty Dancing* movie. He groaned. The innocence of this past week with Izzy was gone. He'd do what Neil said to protect Izzy. With any luck, he'd have some inspiration from above because even without the scuzzball move from Neil, he was more than confused about Izzy, about Knight, and about what he himself really wanted. Mama wanted him to be happy, but he felt like there was a noose tightening around his neck. If only he knew if someone besides Neil was waiting to kick the platform out from underneath his feet.

16

I zzy spent a miserable evening curled up with her laptop, looking at picture after picture of her and Xavier online. There were a lot. She traced his face on the screen, her finger stopping on the dimple. He looked really good to her. Why had he gotten so cryptic and weird on the plane? He obviously hadn't wanted her with him and Mama tonight. Being left out hurt. Dolly and Hailey had always tried to include her, but she'd removed herself and was always on the outside fringe of her family. Seeing pictures of Dolly, Hailey, and her father together always tugged at her heart and made her feel like the child left home alone. That's why she usually stayed far away from social media, but tonight she binged on it.

With Mama and Xavier, she'd felt like the center of their hearts. He'd gained her trust and made her happy like no one ever had. Yet now, Xavier was acting weird with her. He was going to meet with her father, or maybe already had, and that made her sick. When would she finally be rid of her father's influence? It was her fondest dream to be sure. No, that was wrong. Xavier had quickly become her fondest dream, and for some reason he had ditched her.

She put the computer down and went to scavenge the fridge and freezer for food, knowing there wouldn't be anything appealing.

Finally, she pulled out a too-soft apple and a block of Colby cheese. A rap on her door had her shoving the food back in, slamming the fridge door, and grabbing her cinna-mint lip gloss out of her purse. She quickly put some on, rubbing her lips together and fluffing her ponytail before she pulled the door wide.

"X ... Oh." The let down was swift and painful. "Hi, Hailey."

Hailey's perfect face was full of sympathy. "Hello, my beautiful sister. Ice cream?" She held aloft a carton of Extreme Moose Tracks.

"Oh, yes, that looks like the ideal dinner." She ushered her inside and shut the door. "What are you doing alone on a Friday night?"

They walked together into the attached kitchen, and Hailey set the container on the table while Izzy turned to pull out some spoons.

"I had to turn down three dates to go to some dinner with Daddy. As soon as I got done I headed to the store then here. I knew my favorite sister was back in town and needed some chocolate."

Izzy froze with two spoons in her hand. "Why would I *need* some chocolate?"

Hailey bit at her lip. "Well, the, um thing with Xavier."

"What do you know?" Izzy dropped the spoons and grabbed Hailey's arm. "Why was dad meeting with him? What is he doing meddling in my life again?"

"I don't know anything about Daddy and Xavier. I'm talking about the pictures of him having drinks with that supermodel, the Italian one with a chest bigger than my mama's."

"No, you're wrong." Panic fluttered in her chest, but she shoved it away. Xavier wasn't a player. He cared about her. Hadn't he proved how wonderful he was in Mexico? "X was meeting with Dad tonight, and then he was going to his house to eat dinner with his mama."

Hailey studied her for a few seconds, twisted her beautiful mouth, then finally pulled her phone out and tapped on it. Slowly, she turned the phone around. Splayed on the screen was Xavier with Alexandria Fortunata draped all over him. Her arm wrapped tight around his perfect abdomen, her long, bare leg lounging over his. Xavier was leaning toward the supermodel, and it looked like she was whispering to him, and he was clearly smiling, his dimples on display for all.

Her stomach pitched, and Izzy was certain she'd be sick. The caption read, "Xavier Newton moves on from the daughter of Texas Titans' owner to every man's dream woman."

"Are you sure this is tonight?" Her voice squeaked, and she hated herself for it. She'd just been online and hadn't seen it. But then, she'd been focused on the pictures of her and Xavier and hadn't refreshed her feed for a while.

"I'm so sorry, sis."

Cold sweat broke out on her forehead. Xavier. No! She'd trusted him. She'd been falling for him. No, no, no!

Her hands trembled as she pushed the phone back into Hailey's hand. Izzy shook her head and swallowed hard. "It's um ... Not your fault." She couldn't look at her sister. "I'm glad I found out from someone who loves me"—she gestured to the table—"and brings chocolate."

Hailey wrapped her up in a tight hug. Izzy blinked back the tears. She would not cry over him. He'd seemed absolutely perfect, but she'd known from the moment she met him exactly what she was getting into. She'd convinced herself that being around him on their marathon date and in Mexico with the children was his true character. She'd been deluded. His true character had been last Thursday night at the bachelor auction—the hungry wolf who could never be satiated with just one woman. Exactly like her father. Why should she even be surprised? Why did it have to hurt like this?

She kept blinking and miraculously held the moisture in. Hailey pulled back and gave her a brave smile. "'Buck up, little camper. We'll beat this mountain together.'"

Izzy actually laughed at the *Better off Dead* quote.

"What do you say we eat ice cream and watch *Dirty Dancing*?"

Izzy was thrown back to Mexico and dancing with Xavier. The way he'd looked at her, their banter, the way he'd touched her and kissed her. No, no, no. She couldn't go there. Now, he'd not only ruined her trust, but also the memories with her mom of watching what used to be her favorite movie. "Not *Dirty Dancing*."

"*How to Lose a Guy in Ten Days*?"

"How about *Harry Potter*?" A distraction might help, but she couldn't handle any happily ever afters right now.

"I got ya. Romance is out. At least let's do the new *Thor* and have something hot to look at. I'm pretty sure it's on pay-per-view."

"Okay, I can handle that." Izzy's heart had been handed to her on a platter. Ice cream and a movie weren't going to help or change anything, but at least she had Hailey.

17

Izzy woke the next morning feeling like she'd been drugged. Hailey hadn't stayed too long after the movie ended, and when Izzy was alone, the tears had come, and they had come hard. Xavier had seemed so good, so true. How could he do this to her? She wanted to storm over to his house and cuss him up one side and down the other, but her pride wouldn't let her. He'd have to come to her. Sadly, there weren't any messages or missed calls on her phone, voice mail, Instagram, or Snapchat. She'd checked every few minutes throughout the night. Even if he did come to her, could she let him back in? Probably not.

Pulling herself out of bed, she hoped she had the energy to run because that was the only way she was going to feel even marginally better. Somehow, she needed to get into the hospital today and evaluate what she'd missed and be ready to start fresh Monday. She quickly dressed, drank a large glass of water, and forced herself out into the sunshine. It was already warm. Maybe she'd walk for a while and hope her body found the energy to pick up the pace at some point.

She left her gated complex and forced herself to lift her legs into a semi-believable jog along the busy street. She made it half a mile then turned into a nice neighborhood she enjoyed running through. It was quiet and very pretty with large trees and established homes. Izzy slowed to a walk again and just appreciated the shady street, being outside, and that she could move at all after the pity fest she'd consumed last night.

Flashes of Xavier rotated through her mind. How could he have been such a master of deviousness that she hadn't recognized it in him? What had she done that made him ditch her like yesterday's greasy barbecue spare ribs? No, she couldn't think like that. It wasn't her fault any more than it was her mom's fault that her father had deceived her so thoroughly. Her mom's last years had probably been miserable because she trusted the wrong man. At least, Xavier had shown his true colors much quicker than her father had.

Izzy tried to clear her head and admire the huge begonias and clematis lining the walkway of a sprawling rock and stucco home when she heard a car pull up next to her. A door slid open, and she glanced over, instinctively picking up her pace. A gray minivan was idling beside her, and a tall man wearing a ski mask leapt out of the open door. Izzy darted away from him, but he grabbed her arm and yanked her back as a scream ripped from her throat.

"Help!" She hollered at the top of her lungs, hitting at his hand.

He lifted her off her feet and shoved her inside. The rear seats were folded down, and she tumbled against the opposite door. The open door slammed shut, and the man reached for her. Izzy pulled on the handle to open the other door, but it didn't budge.

The man wrapped his hands around her arm and yanked her hands from the door. Izzy whirled and hit him. He grabbed both of her wrists and held them tight. Pain laced through her arms as she felt like her bones were going to snap.

"Just relax, Princess, and you and I will get along just fine."

Tears of frustration and anger rushed to her eyes as she thought of Xavier calling her princess in a smart aleck way, and then it turned tender. Xavier. Would she ever see him again? She steeled her spine. It didn't matter. Xavier was gone, and she had to be the one to rescue herself.

"What do you want?" she asked.

The man's lips and eyes were revealed in the black ski mask. He smiled and inclined his head toward the driver. "We'll get exactly what we want, Princess. Don't worry about us." Pushing her down against the van door, he held onto one of her wrists and settled down next to her. Izzy couldn't catch a breath and could hardly formulate a prayer. Her father had always worried she might get kidnapped, and she'd mocked him about it. How she wished she'd never had to experience the terror that brought icy sweat all over her body.

18

X avier was in his gym pulling through a set of cable rows when his phone rang. He didn't recognize the number, so he ignored it. He finished the tenth rep, and the phone rang again. He should just block the call, but he was grumpy and wanted to tell somebody off. His agent was a pathetic slime ball and Xavier had given in to him to protect Izzy. The mock date with Alexandria last night had been miserable. She wouldn't stop touching him, and he had to look like he enjoyed it for the stupid pictures. Firing his agent after the contract was signed wasn't soon enough, but he couldn't allow him to make Izzy look like a tramp.

He'd arrived home last night to Mama informing him she'd invited Brody and his brothers over because Ace and Kade were both out on dates. Those boys had plowed through every dish she'd set in front of them. So his best friends were happily dating their dream women. His dream woman probably hated him, and he'd had to eat cheese sticks and baby carrots for dinner because his mama was obviously ticked at him.

"What?" he barked into the phone.

"If you want to see Isabella Knight alive again, you will remain on the line and follow my instructions exactly."

His abdomen tightened, and he almost lost his grip on the phone. "How did you get this number?"

"Is that really your top concern right now, or do you want to not find your girl cut into tiny pieces because you didn't listen to me?"

Xavier swallowed hard and talked fast. "I'll do whatever you want. Please don't hurt her."

"I thought that might be your response. Walk straight to your garage and climb in your Land Rover. If you talk to anyone on the way or try to call the police, I will know."

Xavier leapt to his feet and started for the stairs. Mama was still in bed. Could he write her a note? What would he tell her? There's no way they could know if he stopped to write a note, but Mama didn't know how to track his phone and send help. Hopefully the police or one of his friends could. He reached his kitchen and pulled a paper pad and pen out of a kitchen drawer.

"I heard that. Drop the pen and paper and get in your Land Rover."

"How do you know I drive a Land Rover?" But Xavier dropped the pen and paper.

"I know everything, X."

He hurried out of his kitchen entry and into the garage. Jumping into the Land Rover, he pressed on the brake and pushed the start button. His breath was coming hard and fast like he'd run the forty-yard dash twenty times. Punching the garage button, he hated how slowly it clanked out of the way.

"Relax, X. I haven't hurt her, yet."

"What do you want?"

"I'll tell you when you get here. As you exit your neighborhood, drive south."

Xavier followed the man's instructions, turning down one road then back up another for over forty minutes. His palms were sweating, and he couldn't form logical thoughts. Why would somebody kidnap Izzy and call him? But then, who else did she have? If she was being honest with him and wasn't in league with her father, the kidnapper would be pretty smart to go after Xavier instead of her father. Hopefully, it was just about money and they wouldn't hurt Izzy. The comment about cutting her was just to scare him. *Please let it just be about scaring him.*

He finally pulled into an old strip mall. A few of the stores were still in business but not open for the day. The majority of the spaces were vacant.

"Park in front of the third store from the left and walk in. Don't even think about calling 911. I can see you from here. Just come in."

Xavier's heart picked up speed again. He dropped his phone into the pocket of his shorts, climbed out of the vehicle, and cautiously approached the door. Was Izzy even in there? This could be a setup simply to attack him, yet he had to go in. It was Izzy.

He pushed the door hard, and it banged open. He walked inside. The interior was open and swept clean. All he could see was Izzy against the bare wall, bound and gagged.

"Izzy!" He yelled, running toward her.

She was shaking her head desperately, her voice too muffled to understand, and her eyes focused on something behind him. Xavier turned in time to see a tall man wearing a ski mask rushing at him. He threw a punch at Xavier's head. Xavier ducked out of the way, and the man went flying past him. Xavier dove on top of him and slammed his elbow between the guy's shoulder blades. The guy flattened to the concrete floor. Xavier grabbed his shoulders and rolled him over, driving his fist into his face. The guy groaned and cowered.

He heard a shuffle from the corner and glanced up. Was there more than one kidnapper? He would think so, but who knew? Izzy was trying to slide toward him. He wanted to go to her, but he had to make sure this guy, and whoever else was around, wouldn't hurt her first.

The guy slugged him in the abdomen as someone from behind him slammed something hard into his back. He groaned and released his grip. The guy scrambled out from under him, and both men sprinted for the back door. Xavier felt like he should go after them, but he wanted to get to Izzy more. If there were more kidnappers or those two came back, he didn't want to be in a situation similar to the waterfall with the guy holding a knife to Izzy's throat.

Standing, he rushed to her side and dropped onto his knees. His eyes quickly scanned her face and body for injuries, but she looked okay besides the gag and binding, dressed in a tank top and shorts like she'd been out running. He glanced around, wondering if someone else was watching them, waiting to come out and attack. Loosening the gag, he pulled it off. "Is there another guy?"

"Just those two," she said.

Xavier's eyes darted around as he yanked his phone from his pocket. He barely managed to hold his thumb on the button long enough to enable the touch screen and then shakily dialed 911. He quickly explained the situation and gave their location then dropped his phone into his pocket and helped Izzy stand up. "Let's get out of here."

She nodded her agreement. Xavier wrapped his arm around her and ushered her out the front door. She could probably feel him trembling, but he couldn't control it. The anxiety of seeing her bound and gagged and the rush of relief that she was in his arms now were making his entire body shake.

As soon as they were in the bright sunlight and around the back of his Land Rover, semi-hidden from the space she'd been held captive, he turned Izzy around and worked the knot binding her hands together. The adrenaline was fading, but he was still on alert for the tall guy or his partner, so his heart rate wasn't slowing, and he was struggling to steady his hands.

The kidnappers had known the exact moment he would be walking into that office space. Why hadn't they had a knife or gun on Izzy or a better planned attack? They'd double-teamed him then both ran away. Why had they even kidnapped her? They hadn't asked for money or anything. Something was wrong, and nothing was adding up in his brain, but he had Izzy. That was all that mattered right now.

The knot finally came loose, and he dropped the rope and turned her to face him. "Are you sure you're okay?"

She nodded and shook her hands out. She looked small, vulnerable, and so beautiful. Then she slapped him across the face.

"What was that for?" He rubbed at his jaw, more confused than ever. Life used to make sense before he met Izzy Knight.

"Ditching me to go out with Alexandria last night."

"You don't understand—"

Izzy threw her arms around his neck and kissed him with such passion and love he almost lost his footing. He wrapped his arms tight around her and returned the kiss. She pulled away, and they both were short of air.

"What was that for?" he asked.

"Rescuing me."

He couldn't help but grin at how cute she was as all the angst and frustration from last night and this morning slipped away. He wanted to kiss her again, but sirens ripped through the air, and she stepped out of his embrace. Hopefully, the police wouldn't take too long because he had a lot of questions for Isabella Knight. He touched his jaw again. She probably had a few for him too.

———

THE POLICE FINALLY FINISHED THEIR QUESTIONING AND TAKING evidence, what little there was. They typed all of Xavier and Izzy's personal information into a computer and told them they were free to go. They seemed as confused by the thwarted kidnapping attempt as she was. The men hadn't hurt her in any way. They hadn't demanded any money. They hadn't really hurt Xavier, besides the one guy fighting with him. She could still picture Xavier kicking that guy's trash so easily. Xavier was a hero, but also a dipwad. He deserved a couple more slaps, maybe a few more kisses, but she really wished he would explain why he'd been with the model chick last night.

"I'll take you home," Xavier said with little enthusiasm.

"Sorry to be a burden." She tossed back at him.

He opened her door, waited for her to climb in, and walked around to his side. He started the vehicle and drove toward her condo. Neither of them said anything. Izzy was bursting with questions, accusations, and demands, but he wouldn't even look at her, his hand gripping the steering wheel tightly.

Finally, they pulled through the gate and into her condo parking lot. She reached for the door handle. He jumped out and ran around, waiting while she climbed down then shutting the door. They walked silently up to her condo door. She stopped at the door and turned to face him, hating how awkward they were. Was it really just yesterday morning he'd rescued her from being shoved off the waterfall? And now, he'd rescued her again. He was fearless and brave and she knew she was falling for him, but he was also a complete jerk. How could he have ditched her for another woman last night? Why?

Should she thank him for rescuing her? Yes, but she didn't want to start this conversation. She tilted her head up and stared into his dark gaze. He looked as unsettled as her, but angry too. Kind of scary angry.

"I need the truth, Izzy."

"*You* need the truth? Seriously, Xavier?" She tapped her fingers on her arm. "I'll give you the truth. You pretended you cared about me then dumped me like yesterday's garbage and took out some model last night. Is that the truth you're looking for?" Her voice was too loud and she didn't even care.

He brushed a hand through the air like he was swiping away an irritating fly. "Alexandria meant nothing. I went because my agent set it up. I went because ..." His voice faded out and his eyes darted around at the other apartment doors and the cars parked below them. What was he looking for?

"Oh, that makes complete sense. So I shouldn't care that my boyfriend had some beautiful woman draped all over him last night at some bar. No big deal. It was all for your 'agent.'" She made quote marks with her fingers. Had she just called him her boyfriend? That might be taking it too far.

"It meant nothing. I promise." He stared deeply at her as if begging her to see something she didn't understand. "All those women were either setups or encouraged by my agent. It's part of his way to make me look more appealing as a player."

"That's slimy." She couldn't believe Xavier would do that.

"I know, and I hate it. I've always hated it." His eyes swept over her. "You're the only woman I've ever dated that means something to me."

Her heart started to soften. "You lost my trust, X."

He swallowed hard. "I shouldn't have done the pictures, but I promise you that's all it was, pictures."

"You could've called and explained that before I saw it splayed over social media." And had her heart broken in the process.

He cocked his head and studied her. "I should've. I'm sorry, Izzy. I didn't mean to hurt you like that."

She processed his words. They seemed sincere, but yesterday, she'd trusted him above anyone in her life. Today, it was too tender, and she didn't know what to believe.

He lowered his voice and took a step closer. "Look ..." He glanced around again. "I don't know if you'll believe me but I went with Alexandria last night to protect you. My agent is a slime ball and as soon as this contract is signed I'll be done with him."

She was so confused. How was taking pictures with a super model protecting her and why couldn't he just spell it all out? She studied him. "How is that protecting me?"

He shook his head. "My agent threatened ... he was going to make you look bad. I'll explain it all later, but you need to trust me. Can you trust me, Izzy?"

She gnawed at her cheek and finally said, "I don't know."

Xavier flicked his thumb against his pant leg. "Please believe I wouldn't hurt you, Izzy. If you believe anything I say, believe that none of those women meant anything to me, and I'm sorry about the pictures you saw last night."

She studied him and then finally nodded, still not sure if she trusted him or why he couldn't just spell it all out. He leaned closer and said quietly, "Can I trust you?"

"What?" She stepped away from him.

"I can't trust your father or my agent, but I really wish I knew if I could trust you."

She bristled and wanted to smack him. "What are you talking about? This is all about me trusting you, not the other way around!"

"Why did you buy me at the bachelor auction?"

She gritted her teeth. Why were they back to this? "I told you, to get money for the hospital."

"But why would your dad be that generous with you?"

"Maybe he actually cares." It hurt to say it because she didn't believe it and probably never would. "Why do you care if he donates money to my hospital?"

"I care because I think he's trying to manipulate me. I think your dad set this whole thing up so I'd stay in Dallas."

She fell back a step. "Excuse me?"

"He wanted us to date. He knew how appealing you would be to me, and he wanted us to fall in love so I wouldn't take Denver's offer."

For some reason, instead of listening to his twisted logic about her father's scheming, which she didn't actually doubt because her father would do anything for his Titans, she focused on three words. "Fall in love?"

Xavier paused for half a beat, a hungry look coming over his face, hungry for her, but it was there and gone quickly. He shook his head and muttered, "Even your kidnapping today seemed contrived. They didn't want anything. The guy fighting me was pathetic, and then he got out of there as quick as possible. Would your dad set something like that up?"

"Why would he do that?" She didn't have a good relationship with her father, but he didn't hate her enough to have somebody kidnap her. Did he?

"To bring us back together. To keep me here."

She couldn't even compute what he was saying. "You're trying to tell me that my dad *used* me to lure you into staying?"

"Did he?"

"How would I know?" She shoved her hair behind her ear.

He took a step closer. "You tell me. Did you make up all the stuff you shared with me, all the hatred with your father? Are you in league with him to keep me away from Denver?"

She slapped him across the face, harder than she had the previous two times.

Xavier's eyes hardened and darkened. "The last two times you slapped me I at least got a kiss out of the deal."

"Don't plan on it," she shot back at him. He'd betrayed her trust and hurt her without a very good explanation and now he was claiming she was in league with her father?

He took a step closer, and she backed up a step, running into the door. His smell overwhelmed her, not his usual cologne but a clean, manly scent she couldn't hide from.

"Tell me the truth, Izzy. Was it all a ploy?"

"If you can believe what your twisted little mind is telling you, then you don't know me at all."

"The only thing I know is you're the most beautiful enchantress I've ever met."

She glared up at him. His words should've been kind, but they were twisted to make it look like she'd put a spell on him or something. "I am not some enchantress, and I haven't done anything my father has wanted since I was ten. Why would I care about his stupid football team or try to *tempt* you to stay?"

He planted his hands on either side of her head and leaned in. "You tell me, Princess, because I'm more confused than I've ever been in my life."

"I am *not* a Princess." She yelled at him.

Xavier bent down and kissed her. The kiss was possessive and strong and took her breath away. Unfortunately, her body reacted, and she cupped his face with her hands, stood on tiptoes, and deepened the kiss. Xavier crushed her against him, taking the kiss to levels daydreams were made of. His hands were warm on the bare skin of her shoulders and almost as demanding as his lips. He wanted her, all of her. Could she trust him again?

After who knew how long, he pulled back and muttered, "You sure don't kiss like a princess."

That was his response? She needed reassurance of love and trust, and he mocked her? Izzy planted her hands on his chest and tried to shove him away, but he didn't budge. "Go to Denver!" She screamed. "See if I care."

She whirled and pulled her key out of the small pocket in her shorts, working it in with trembling fingers. Xavier's presence still surrounded her—his breath, his smell, his touch from a few seconds ago. She had to get inside before she lost it completely. The lock finally turned and she pushed the door open. Xavier's hands dropped away, and she didn't allow herself to look at him as she slipped inside and slammed the door.

Leaning against the door, she touched her lips and let the tears slide down her face. At least she had other kisses to remember him by because the last one was amazing, but it wasn't her X. She sighed. He'd never be her X again.

19

X avier stared at Izzy's door. He shouldn't have kissed her like that, like he wanted to possess her, not like he cared about her. Especially with her having a hard time trusting him because of all the crap with his agent. He wanted to knock on the door and apologize, but she had slapped him, again, and yelled at him to go to Denver. Most importantly, he still didn't know who or what to believe. Would Knight really go to such extremes to keep him here? Xavier actually wanted to stay here and be with his friends, but Izzy ripping out his heart like this made him want to commit to Denver.

He stomped off her patio and down the steps, driving much too quickly to his house. When he stormed inside, his mama was cooking omelets in the kitchen.

"Are those actually for me, or are you feeding them to Brody and his brothers?"

She arched an eyebrow. "I don't need your sass, boy."

Xavier sank onto a barstool. "I'm sorry, Mama."

"Were you out on a run?"

"No. Izzy was kidnapped."

"What!" Mama dropped an egg on the slate floor. It broke open and oozed out, but she didn't move to pick it up.

"She's okay now. I rescued her." He rolled his eyes. "Whole fat lot of good it did me."

"Who kidnapped her? Why?"

"That's the thing." He pushed a hand over his short hair. "I don't know who or why. The police were just as confused." He shook his head and tried to explain. "I got a phone call from some guy this morning, saying he had Izzy. I followed his instructions. When I got there, Izzy was tied up and this guy fought with me, but everything about the situation was off. Like the fight was staged. When another guy hit me from behind, I let the first guy go, and they both ran off. They didn't ask for money or try to hurt either of us." He tapped his thumb against his leg.

Mama stared at him as the onions, peppers, mushrooms, and sausage sizzled and popped in the pan. It smelled really good. "You think it was a setup?"

"But why would she do that?" Xavier leaned forward against the counter—confused and tired and missing Izzy already.

"I don't understand how you think our sweet Izzy would set up her own kidnapping."

He tapped his palm on the counter. "I agree. She wouldn't do that. But something stinks here. I think it was her father."

"Messed up family," she muttered.

"I don't think we have any idea." He shook his head. "Let's head to Denver today instead of tomorrow."

"Is Izzy coming with us?"

"No."

"Why not?" Her eyes filled with a challenge that he had never stepped up to.

"Oh, Mama." He buried his head in his hands. "Let's not get into this right now. I've got a huge headache, and I'm hungry." He should tell his mama about the crap his agent had pulled, but she'd be outraged and probably call Neil out on national television or something and Xavier would be in a bigger mess than he was in now.

"You listen to me," Mama said. "You love that girl, and you need to make it right. I saw your stupid Instagram post with some fakey model chick last night. You probably broke Izzy's heart, and you need to fix it!"

"Mama. You know how much I love you, but I am done with you bossing me around. I'm not going to be with Izzy." Saying the words shredded a piece of his heart. His agent had messed things up with him and Izzy but so had Izzy's dad and everything was a convoluted mess in his head.

"Recognizing you love Izzy does not mean I'm bossing you around, little boy."

"I'm not a little boy anymore Mama. I'm a man. We're going to Denver, and I'm probably going to accept their contract and move there, and what I'd really appreciate is you not bringing her name up again."

"Why not?" She jammed her hands onto her hips.

"Because it hurts!" He glanced down at the granite countertop, running his hand along the rough edge. "It hurts okay. You never talk about my father. Why?"

She reared back, and her eyes widened.

"Why?" Xavier asked quietly.

"Because it hurts."

"So you understand?"

She didn't answer, simply opened her arms. Xavier walked around the bar and held his mama close. The veggies and sausage for the omelet burned in the pan as Mama clung to him. He couldn't imagine the pain she'd been through, losing her husband and raising him on his own. The hurt from losing Izzy wasn't comparable, but it still yanked him inside out and made it hard to keep putting one foot in front of the other. But the hug actually did help with the hurt a little bit.

20

Izzy had no clue if there was any truth to Xavier's theories, but she had to know if her father could do something like this to her. She pulled into the circle drive of her family mansion, but her phone rang before she could open the door.

"Hello," she said cautiously, not recognizing the number.

"Sweet girl," Mama sounded out of breath.

"Oh, Mama." Izzy sighed and leaned her head back against the headrest. She missed Mama so much. She missed Mama's son more.

"Listen, I overheard X arguing with his agent this morning when he was unloading his suitcase upstairs and he thought I was at the store."

"His agent?" He'd said his agent was a slimeball and made him take all those pictures with girls, but he'd still accused her of being in league with her father.

"From what I can gather he only took those pictures with the model chick to protect you from his agent leaking all kinds of mean stuff about you. His agent is making him do all of this nonsense to get more money out of Denver or your daddy."

He'd claimed he was protecting her, but even if she could forget about the pictures with Alexandria why did he keep attacking her and acting like she was in league with her father? "Does he really believe that I only dated him to keep him in Dallas?" she asked.

"If he does I'll kick his hind end," Mama huffed. "No one could doubt your sincerity, sweet girl. And no one with a brain could miss the love you have for my boy."

Izzy's heart thudded irregularly. She did love Xavier and it sounded like he was in a mess. She glanced up at the stucco exterior of the mansion. Maybe she could get to the bottom of this.

"I've got to go," Mama said. "Please don't give up on my boy."

The line went dead and Izzy stared at her phone for a few seconds then dropped it on the console and stomped into her family mansion, startling their butler, Gary, who greeted her with, "Oh, hello, Miss Knight. Your stepmother and sister are not home presently." She never came here when her father was home.

"I know. They're off shopping." She turned to the right and yanked open the office door.

"Miss Knight!" Gary protested.

Her father's head jerked up, and he smiled. "Izzy. Hello, sweetheart." He stood and opened his arms. As if she'd walk into them for a hug. She hadn't done that in over ten years.

She slammed the door behind her and then stomped up to his desk. "Why did you use me to keep Xavier here?"

"What are you talking about?" He finally lowered his arms, realizing no hug was coming, smart man.

"You set up the whole thing, me buying him at the auction, me being kidnapped, all so he wouldn't leave the Titans."

"No, love. I did it for you."

Izzy took a step back. It was true. Everything Xavier had thrown at her was true. She recoiled quickly, planting her hands on the desk. "*Don't* call me love. You don't love anybody but money and football."

"Oh, Izzy." Her father dropped his head. "If only you could see how much I love you. I did all of this for you."

"You tricked me into buying Xavier and then had me kidnapped because you love me?" She folded her arms under her chest. "You're insane."

His eyes met hers, begging. "Sweetheart."

"Don't." She warned him, holding up a hand. She'd never been his sweetheart.

"Just please listen to me."

Izzy waited half a beat before giving him a slight nod.

"Your mother made me promise before she passed that, when the time was right, I would help you find someone wonderful to share your life with."

She flinched, wondering if there was any truth to what he was saying. It seemed like something her mom would do.

"When I first met Xavier, I had a really good feeling about him. I've watched him these past few years, and the kid has character and grit. I like him, and I thought he was perfect for you."

Izzy agreed, and for some reason, it warmed her inside to know that her father approved of Xavier, even though she'd never given much credence to her father's opinions.

"When he got the offer to go to Denver, I didn't want to let him go, but I didn't know how to keep him here. Denver is his hometown, and his mother's there. Maybe it was right to let him go. I was praying about it one night."

"Wait a minute." Izzy raised a hand. "You pray?"

"Of course, I pray." His brows lowered. "I taught you to pray."

"Yeah, and I thought you were the biggest hypocrite on Earth."

He nodded and then swallowed before saying, "I can understand that. I know I deserted you when your mom was sick and after she died, but please understand how hard it was for me to watch her suffer and then to lose her. I was a mess and you look so much like her, it about killed me to see you—"

Izzy did not want to get into this with her father. All of her resentment and anger bubbled below the surface. "Just tell me about Xavier."

He studied her then said, "I'm so sorry I detached from you. I loved your mother desperately, and I fell apart. She was my entire world."

"You *cheated* on her when she was sick." Izzy exploded. "Don't give me that crap about her being your world."

"I ... cheated?" His brow furrowed. "I never cheated on anyone."

Liar! She wanted to scream. The proof was her sister. "Hailey" was all she said.

His mouth flapped open. He swiped a hand over his face and then shook his head. "All these years, you thought Hailey was mine?"

"Of course she's yours." She hated the way he was looking at her, like she was delusional or something. "I saw you hugging Dolly in the kitchen when my mom was sick and you were going in for a kiss."

He opened his mouth but she wasn't finished.

"After Mom died and I understood what cheating was, I started hearing it everywhere, how you and Dolly were together while my mom was still alive. It was only three years after Mom was gone that you married Dolly, and I heard the talk all the time about how you'd been with Dolly and that Hailey was your daughter. That's why you moved them in next door when Mom got sick."

"Oh, sweetheart. All these years, why didn't you just ask me or Dolly? Hailey isn't mine. Yes, she calls me daddy, but that's because I asked her to when I adopted her. I love her like she's my own, but she's not mine." He blew out a breath.

"I asked Hailey about it once and she said she was my sister and you were her daddy."

He smiled kindly. "Of course she did, Hailey idolizes you and wanted you to be sisters in every way."

Izzy realized that was true and Hailey had been a young teenager at the time.

"Why didn't you ask Dolly or I?"

"You and I haven't had much of a relationship and it was a bit of an awkward question to ask Dolly."

He nodded his understanding. "I'm sorry again that I withdrew from you after I lost Mariana."

There wasn't really anything she could say to that. He'd deserted her when she needed him the most. She didn't know that the pain would ever go away, but she appreciated him trying to apologize.

"I was faithful to your mother, Izzy." He kind of flinched when he said it and rushed on to explain. "When Dolly moved in next door, she and her husband were having trouble, and truthfully, we were both lonely, and it was hard to keep proper boundaries, but we were just very good friends for the first six years I knew her. Three years while your mother fought the cancer and then for the three years after, while I mourned and I shut you out. Then I had no clue how to open your heart to me again and honestly seeing you ripped me apart so I did stay away from you. Dolly became my best friend before I fell in love with her. We were close enough that I can see how the rumors would start, but I promise I was faithful to your mom. I had absolutely no clue you thought I'd cheated."

She couldn't comprehend all of this, so she just stared. She'd been too young to understand any of this when her mom first got sick, maybe six or seven. By the time her mom died a few years later, she started hearing the rumors about her dad and Dolly having an affair while her mom was sick and the hug she'd seen in the kitchen solidified it. She didn't comprehend what cheating meant until she was a teenager and her dad married the woman she'd always heard he cheated with.

He barked a laugh. "If you saw me hugging Dolly in our kitchen I'm not surprised. It was hard to keep proper boundaries with her natural exuberance and love for everyone. That woman hugs everybody." He smiled, and Izzy had a little insight into why her mom and Dolly could both love him. He had a nice smile, but he also had love shining in his eyes. He loved Dolly. She'd always known that, but it had always felt like this awful slight to her mom. Yet if all of this was true, he'd loved her mother too, and he and Dolly had done things the right way and had a right to be happy.

"Dolly is a dose of sunshine. That's for sure." Izzy admitted.

"Yes, she is." Her father agreed.

"So, Hailey isn't my sister?" That thought hit her hard. She loved Hailey, and although she'd hated thinking about her father cheating to create her sister, she loved having a sister.

He looked at her incredulously. "I just can't understand what would make you think that."

"I told you I overheard some of the kitchen help saying she was and Hailey claimed she was."

"Sweetheart. I didn't even know Dolly until they moved in next door and Hailey was already three or four at that point. Don't you remember her dad?"

"No. He deserted them, right?"

Her father nodded. "But if you'd ever seen him, he looked so much like Hailey—tall, blonde, blue eyes, straight nose, and the cleft in the chin." He shook his head. "He was a pretty boy. I always wondered what Mariana or Dolly saw in me."

Izzy bit at her lip. "I've thought the same thing."

"I bet you have." He smiled. "Even though you and Hailey aren't sisters by blood, the two of you are sisters," he said.

She nodded. That was true. She adored Hailey. "Why didn't you tell me all of this years ago?"

"I had no idea you had everything so confused in your head." He gave her a gentle smile. "When your mother died, I was such a mess. I could only deal with one day at a time, and you were this beautiful ten-year-old girl I didn't really know how to relate to and it killed me to be around you and think of Mariana nonstop. When I finally started healing and fell in love with Dolly, I wanted to be there for you, but you hated me."

"I don't know if hate is a strong enough word."

"True." He nodded. "We should've healed together, but instead, I turned to my work and thought you were just going through mourning for your mom and teenage girl stuff and would come around. But you never came around, and then you left home as soon as you could." He hung his head. "It about killed me, but at least, I knew you had Dolly and Hailey. I didn't want to push you away from them as well, so I just tried to stay back. But oh, sweetheart, I've missed you. It's an ache that never goes away."

Izzy felt tears spring to her eyes. Her father truly cared about her. This man she'd made out to be a monster cared enough that he'd adopted Hailey when her own father had deserted her. She loved her sister and stepmom so much, and sadly, she'd made her father out to be the villain and shoved him away time and time again. She wanted to hug him and say sorry, but first she had to know.

"The deal with Xavier?"

He sort of bowed his head. "I watched you succeed at your career, so hard-working and driven, not wanting any help from me, from any man, and I knew because of how much you hated me, you wouldn't let yourself fall in love."

Izzy nodded. There was no use denying it.

"So when I prayed, Mariana came to me in a dream and told me Xavier was the one for you."

Izzy gasped and felt a warmth flood over her. Xavier. She'd seen her mother when she'd almost drowned but had chosen Xavier instead.

"At first, it worried me because his agent had painted him as a ladies' man. I don't know how I know, but that's not the real him."

Izzy blinked quickly. Her dad believed in Xavier, her mom wanted them together, and Xavier and his mama claimed he only took those pictures with Alexandria to protect Izzy from his agent. It was all coming at her pretty quick.

"Do you know what his name means?" her dad asked.

She shook her head, thinking it was a warrior of light or something. That would make sense.

"Leader of the resistance, but his true wish is for a wife, children, and a planet that isn't exploding."

Izzy half-laughed. "You got that off an X-Men comic book." How had she forgotten that her business-minded father loved the X-Men?

He nodded and smiled. "Still, isn't that him? He's a fighter and is absolutely fearless on the field, but his heart is still at home. Look how he cares for his mama and for children around the world. I knew he was the one for you, and so I schemed to get you two together."

She regarded him for a few seconds. "You're telling me all this crazy scheming had nothing to do with keeping him in Dallas for your Titans?"

He shrugged and gave her half a grin. "Hey, if I can keep the Triple Threat together, I'll be a happy man." He winked. "But no, sweetheart. I wanted you to be happy. I'm truly sorry about the kidnapping thing. That was Dolly's idea. She thought it would be 'so romantic' when Xavier saved you, and you know I can't tell that woman no."

Oh, Dolly. Izzy loved her so much, but she was quite the romantic airhead sometimes. "That was a horrible idea. I can't believe you went with it."

"You're right. I shouldn't have." He shrugged and seemed very unconcerned.

"You're going to have to clear it up with the police." Her chest tightened. How would the police respond? How had her parents schemed up such a stupid idea to bring her and Xavier together? Her parents. She'd just thought of her dad and Dolly as her parents.

"I know." His wrinkles deepened. "Hopefully, we won't get charged for faking a crime or something, but it would be worth it to show you how much I love you." His eyes were soft and begging her to believe him.

"You're crazy." She felt warm all over, realizing her father did love her as much as he loved Dolly and Hailey. "Can you imagine the publicity if you and Dolly got thrown in jail?"

"I'd take the rap for it. Dolly would never survive without her Frappuccino and hair dryer." He winked.

"You'd go to prison for me and to protect Dolly?" She was dumbfounded that he seemed so unconcerned about the possibility of the police charging him with something and that he truly loved her and Dolly this strongly.

"Of course. It would all be worth it if you find the person who makes you happy like your mother and Dolly have made me."

Izzy couldn't resist any longer. She walked around the desk and threw herself into her daddy's arms. He wrapped her up tight and held her. She hadn't allowed him to hug her since she was eight years old, and it felt like home, a home she'd missed without even realizing it. He smelled of peppermint and coffee and she loved that his smell was still the same.

"Thank you, Daddy," she whispered, her tears wetting his suit coat.

"Oh, Izzy, sweetheart. I love you so much." His voice caught, and his own tears dropped into her hair.

For the first time in years, she believed him.

21

It was good to be back in Denver. Xavier still hadn't decided which contract to sign, especially when Denver had offered six million dollars above Knight's offer. Which had made Neil ecstatic, crowing about how he knew the date with Alexandria would clinch it all for them. Xavier walked away before he slugged him.

Luckily, he was busy at home. Mama always had somebody or some organization she was helping, and as soon as the neighborhood boys got wind Xavier was home, they came over for football.

Xavier came rushing into the kitchen from outside, hot and thirsty. Mama was whipping up a batch of cookies. He pinched a bit of dough.

"Oh, you stop that."

He grinned.

"You doing okay?" she asked.

"No. The boys and I need some homemade strawberry lemonade, and nobody makes it as good as you."

She laughed. "You little manipulator. You know I'd do anything you ask."

"I know."

Her eyes got serious, and she said, "Will you do anything I ask?"

Xavier grabbed a water bottle out of the fridge, opened it, and took a long swallow. "I always try to." He finally answered, dreading where she would go with this.

"Call Izzy."

He shook his head and hurried to take another drink.

"But love, you always obey me because you love me."

"Yeah." He did love her, but he couldn't call Izzy. His mom hadn't been there Saturday morning. She didn't know how it ended. He still didn't know what parts Knight was behind and what parts were real or contrived.

"Shouldn't you obey Izzy for the same reason?"

"You think I love Izzy?"

"I watched you together. I think you love her the way a man should love a woman."

He stared into his mama's deep brown eyes, so full of love, understanding, and hope. He couldn't hide from those eyes. "You're probably right, but she's not the Izzy I fell in love with. I can't trust her or her father, and you can't build love without trust." He'd also broken Izzy's trust when he met up with Alexandria. No matter if he had done it to protect her from his agent's slimy ideas. They couldn't heal from wounds this big.

Mama bit at her lip and simply studied him for a few seconds. "One thing I've learned in this long life is things aren't always as they seem."

Xavier shrugged, not ready to commit either way. "But sometimes they are."

Izzy walked off the plane, happy to be able to stand and walk the stiffness out of her legs. She dialed the number with trembling fingers. "Mama Newton?"

She heard a shriek then Mama said, "Is this my sweet girl?"

"Yes." Izzy laughed, but it was uneasy. "Is X right there?"

"No, he's out in the yard throwing a ball with some boys."

Izzy could picture it, and she wanted to be there watching him.

"Are you going to come and fix my boy's heart, sweet girl?"

"Oh, Mama, I want to." She gripped the phone tightly.

"Well then, get your skinny buns on a plane."

"I just landed in Denver."

"Hallelujah!" Mama screamed into her ear.

Izzy laughed. Her body relaxed. If only Xavier would give her as warm of a reception as Mama. "I just need your address."

"I'll text it to you, and I'll have some of my famous chocolate chip cookies waiting."

"Thank you, Mama. Please don't tell him I'm coming. I need to talk to him face-to-face."

"Well hurry then. I can't stand watching him hurt any longer."

Hearing that made her hurt. "I'm on my way." She hung up and pulled up the Uber app.

22

Xavier caught the ball then fired it back at Marcos. The boy got drilled in the gut, but he was grinning as he wrapped the ball up. Xavier rushed him. Marcos let out a squeak and took off running. Xavier had been able to buy the neighbor's house when it was condemned and knock it down, making a huge side and backyard for Mama. He had also used the space to extend her house when he paid to have it remodeled. Luckily, the local gangs respected him and Mama and hadn't made any trouble for her being in this rundown neighborhood with a bigger and nicer house and yard.

He caught the little man easily and lifted him up in the air. Marcos' laughter pealed through the backyard. Xavier dropped to his knees and pretended to pin the boy down while Marcos giggled and struggled to be free. All the other boys had gone home for the night, but Marcos' mom was working late again.

"You're down," Xavier said.

"Let's do it again, X!"

Xavier was so happy to be with Marcos, and his fears about the boy had been put to rest. He was listening to Mama's advice and told Xavier that he was going to stay far away from gangs and drugs so he could play football when he grew up. He'd also made some friends at school who were good kids, and their families seemed to be taking an interest in the cute little man and inviting him to their homes often. His mom was trying hard to be more involved and make sure he was either at Mama's or another safe spot when she couldn't be home.

A movement on the back patio caught Xavier's eye as he stood and offered the little man a hand up. "Maybe Mama has some cookies and more lemonade for us."

Mama was indeed carrying a pitcher of lemonade, but trailing behind her with a plate of cookies and the paper cups was Izzy. Her dark, shiny hair trailed down across her shoulder. Her smile appeared a little uncertain to him, but she looked so beautiful in her floral print sundress he wanted to run and swoop her off the ground. As much as part of him wanted to do that, he didn't move. He was frozen to the grass and had no clue what to do or think.

They sat everything down on the patio table, and Mama said, "Marcos, this is my friend Izzy."

"Hi, beautiful lady." Marcos pumped his eyebrows.

Mama and Izzy laughed. All Xavier could do was stare at her. Why had she come? What did this mean for them?

"Grab a couple of cookies. Then you and I are going to go in and watch YouTube videos of the Triple Threat."

"Sweet!" Marcos grabbed as many cookies as he could fit in his hand and trotted to Mama's side.

"Be sweet with my girl." Mama admonished Xavier before taking Marcos' free hand and walking inside.

Xavier nodded, completely focused on Izzy's deep brown eyes. She finally looked at him, and it was all he could do to not grab her and kiss her like he'd done on her doorstep after she'd been kidnapped.

She tucked her hair behind her ear and whispered, "Hello, X."

Xavier's feet started to work, and he crossed the distance separating them, stopping a foot away. "Why did you come?" It was too harsh and probably not the best opening line, but he couldn't handle any crap right now. He needed her in his life. He'd go to Dallas for less money if she wanted him. Could they really make it work?

Her eyes flickered over his face, settling on his lips for a beat before she met his gaze and gave him a slow smile. "I came because every time I slapped you I'd also given you a kiss, and I owe you for that last slap."

His brow furrowed. "You gave me a kiss the last time too. You don't owe me anything." Though he'd happily take a slap across the cheek if he could kiss her again.

"No, *you* kissed *me.*" She stepped so close he could smell her sweet gardenia scent.

His breath shortened. "So you came here to make it right?"

She placed her palms on his chest, and the oxygen was stripped from his lungs.

"I came here to make a lot of things right."

Xavier knew they had a lot of talking to do, but he couldn't resist wrapping his arms around the small of her back and bringing her body flush to his. She gave a cute little gasp. He bent down and captured her lips, kissing her long and good. He drew back and said, "I still have some questions."

"I'm sure you do, but the score's not even. I haven't kissed *you* yet."

Xavier grinned and winked at her. "I'm waiting."

She rose up on tiptoes and took control of his lips in a way no woman had ever done. Xavier didn't want the kiss to ever end. Several wonderful minutes of silent communication had his nerve endings singing, and he wanted more of this incredible woman.

Regrettably, she fell back onto her heels, stepped out of his arms and took his hand. "Mama said cookies and lemonade would sweeten you up so you'd listen to what I had to say."

"You don't need either of those when you've got lips like yours."

Izzy chuckled. They sank into chairs, and he poured them both a glass of lemonade, taking a long drink.

Izzy turned to him, and their knees touched. He couldn't resist putting his hand on her bare knee. She smiled.

"X, you were right about my father."

"He was trying to coerce me into staying with the Titans?"

"Yes, but not for the reason you think."

Xavier squeezed her leg and sat back in his chair. He didn't need the distraction of touching that smooth skin to hear what would probably be a sordid story. He just hoped Izzy fit into the tale in a way that wouldn't pull her away from him again.

"He actually cares about me."

Xavier was glad to hear that she believed that and hoped it was true.

"He didn't cheat on my mother and he loves me, Dolly, and Hailey, and Hailey isn't my half-sister. She's my stepsister."

"Wait?" He raised a hand. "You thought she was your half-sister?"

"Yeah."

"You look nothing alike."

"Ha. Thank you very much."

Xavier looked at her very seriously. "I've already told you, Izzy, that you're the most beautiful woman in the world to me, and I want to tell you one more time that I am very sorry about the stupid pictures with Alexandria. My agent blackmailed me but I'm done listening to him. If you can promise to not believe the media if my agent releases some sordid, but doctored pictures of me and tries to run your name through the mud, I promise you I'll never let him manipulate me again."

"I trust you, X."

"Thank you." He smiled at her then turned the subject back. "Your father?"

She took a deep breath and pressed her palms together. "What it comes down to is my father did try to manipulate us together, but he did it because he loves me, and he thinks you're terrific. He wants me to be happy and believes you are the man for me."

Xavier simply blinked at her. Her father wanted them together because he cared for them, not for his Titans? "How can you be sure that he didn't do it for his team?"

Izzy leaned against him, and his arm automatically came around her. She looked up at him, and those dark eyelashes framed her eyes so perfectly. "Because I could see the love in his eyes, just like I can see the love in yours."

"How can you be sure that I'm the one for you?" His voice deepened.

"I think you can convince me by kissing me again."

Xavier bent down and gave her a chaste kiss on the lips, but it wasn't enough. It wasn't nearly enough. He wrapped his hands around her waist and lifted her onto his lap. Izzy gasped but recovered quickly, framing his face with her hands and deepening the kiss. Xavier groaned and pulled her in tight to him. If this kiss didn't convince her she was the one for him, he'd just have to keep kissing her, and that sounded more important and worthwhile to him than any contract negotiation or football career.

EPILOGUE

Izzy and Xavier were in his basement theater room, snuggling on the couch. With his musky scent and strong arms surrounding her, she couldn't imagine ever being happier. The music came on at the end of *Dirty Dancing*, and she sighed, content and happy.

Xavier stood and held out his hands. "Would you like to dance?"

Izzy placed both of her hands in his and let him tug her up. They moved away from the couch and ottoman, and he cradled her hand against his chest and wrapped his other arm around the small of her back. They swayed back and forth for a little while. Then Xavier surprised her, swinging her out then back into his chest. She laughed as she bumped against him.

"Hey, that was just like the movie," he said.

"You want to recreate more of the movie?" Her heart beat a little faster.

"Oh, yes, ma'am. Now that I've watched it a few dozen times, I can do every move Johnny tried to do."

"A few dozen." She scoffed. "Twice, you've watched it twice."

"True, but I still say you do that lay back swoopy move way better than Baby."

Izzy laughed again as Xavier wrapped his hands around her waist and whispered, "Please."

How could she resist that? She leaned back and swooped a low circle back bend. When she came back up to face him, he grinned and picked her up off her feet and above his head. Her stomach leapt and she laughed happily. She almost touched the ceiling as she straightened her body, and he spun a slow circle. The next part was her favorite as he lowered her until she was flush against him.

She put a hand on his face, touching one of his dimples. "Man, I love these things."

Xavier bent and kissed her softly. "Man, I love these things."

Izzy stood on tiptoes and returned the kiss. Joy, safety, and desire encompassed her as his lips tenderly caressed hers. When he deepened the kiss, she couldn't help but moan as pleasure receptors went off all over her body. She wrapped her hands around his neck and held on.

A stream of water hit her square in the face. Izzy cried out, and Xavier quickly tried to shelter her with his body, but the water was coming from every direction. Ace, Kade, and Brody each had a water gun and were dousing them. She suspected Brody's little brothers were somewhere joining in the attack, but she couldn't see them as she blinked to try to clear her eyes then got hit in the face again.

Xavier growled and ran at Kade first, ripping the gun from his hands and then turning it on Ace. They all laughed like a bunch of little boys. Seconds later, everyone but Xavier scampered toward the stairs, their assault successful. A door slammed upstairs, and they were gone.

Izzy stood there, dripping. Xavier turned to her, water streaming down his face. "I'm sorry. They're a bunch of crazy idiots."

Laughter bubbled out of Izzy. Xavier chuckled too, wiping his face with his hand.

"You've got to admit that was pretty funny."

"It was." He hurried to the bathroom and returned with a couple of towels. Izzy wiped her face and arms. There was no hope for drying her shirt.

Xavier dropped his towel on the couch and turned to her. Her pulse skyrocketed at the intent look in his eyes. "It would've been funny if they hadn't interrupted the best part of my day."

"Oh? And how can you call it the best when you do it several dozen times a day."

"Ah! That's not fair. I'm lucky to get as much kissing in as the number of times you claim I've watched *Dirty Dancing*."

He reached her and trailed a hand down her face and along her arm, taking her hand in his and whirling her around so she was facing away from him. He lifted her arm up and then trailed his fingers down the side of her abdomen.

Izzy shivered, trickles of pleasure washing over her. "I think you've watched *Dirty Dancing* plenty."

He bent down. "As long as you don't claim I've kissed you plenty."

"Never."

Xavier kissed her cheek tenderly then pulled a small box out of his pocket and held it out in front of her.

Izzy gasped. He opened the red velvet box, revealing an exquisite tear drop diamond set against white gold. Izzy fell in love all over again.

"If I give you this, do I get to kiss you any time I want to?" Xavier asked in a low, husky tone.

"I think you have to get brave enough to pop the question first."

Xavier spun her to face him, staring down at her. "I don't know if I'm that brave."

"My father claims you're fearless on the field and off."

Xavier chuckled. "Well, he's kind of a big fan of mine."

"His daughter's a bigger fan. Wait. Did you already ask him for my hand?"

"Yes." He grinned, and his beautiful dimples were on fine display.

"And?"

"And he gave me his blessing and forced me to sign a sixty-eight million dollar contract."

Izzy had heard all about how they'd also confronted Xavier's agent together and with the commissioner listening in. Neil would never work in the entertainment industry again.

Izzy arched her eyebrows. "Guess he wants to make sure you can take care of his little girl."

"Oh, I can take care of her all right." He bent his head and claimed her lips with his until her heart was thrumming in her neck. "Izzy?" he whispered against her lips.

"Yes?" she whispered back.

"Marry me, and make me the happiest man on the planet?"

She smiled. "I didn't realize you'd turn this into a cheese fest."

He chuckled. "Marry me, and I will worship you for all eternity."

"Oh, brother. Give me the ring."

Xavier pulled it out of the box and slid it onto her finger. She smiled up at him. "I love you, X. Marry me, and I'll teach you moves that put Johnny and Baby to shame."

"Now, that sounds like a plan." He lifted her off her feet and swung her in a circle. Then he set her back down and kissed her. The kiss was tender and slow, yet her lips sung with the passion and excitement of his touch. Izzy was going to plan a very short engagement, but at this moment, all she could focus on was their connection. His strong arms surrounded her, and his lips eradicated all rational thought. She was transported to heaven with Xavier and knew her father had been right about his name. He could win any battle but longed for a wife and family and a world that wasn't exploding. She would give him her all, and he'd give her even more in return—true joy and him by her side.

ABOUT THE AUTHOR

Cami is a part-time author, part-time exercise consultant, part-time housekeeper, full-time wife, and overtime mother of four adorable boys. Sleep and relaxation are fond memories. She's never been happier.

Go to www.camichecketts.com to sign up for Cami's newsletter to receive a free ebook copy of *The Feisty One: A Billionaire Bride Pact Romance* and information about new releases, discounts, and promotions.

www.camichecketts.com
cami@camichecketts.com

ALSO BY CAMI CHECKETTS

Made in the USA
San Bernardino, CA
19 March 2018